Once burned by love, Second Lieutenant Dawn Winters vows she'll never surrender her heart again. That is, until an unfortunate collision with Drew Sunrise forces her to reconnoiter and gather her forces. Not only must she battle the coronavirus pandemic — her latest mission — but she also has to combat Drew's sexy appeal and charm.

Drew Sunrise, single and never married, is concerned with two things, raising his teenage niece while her mother fights in Afghanistan, and his passion for work. When Dawn bumps into his truck — literally, with her car — the attraction is instant, and he can't help falling victim to his growing feelings for her. He doesn't need the added struggles life decides to throw his way.

Can these two work past the worries in their lives and form a perfect union, or will they lose the peace that lasting love can bring?

This book is a work of fiction. Names, characters, places, and incidents either are products of the author's imagination or are used fictitiously. Any resemblance to actual events or locales or persons, living or dead, is entirely coincidental.

Mountain Fever
Copyright © 2021 Kathy Kalmar
ISBN: 978-1-4874-3217-1
Cover art by Martine Jardin

Published by eXtasy Books Inc or
Devine Destinies, an imprint of eXtasy Books Inc

Look for us online at:
www.eXtasybooks.com or www.devinedestinies.com

Mountain Fever
Mountain Series 14

By

Kathy Kalmar

DEDICATION

To Larry, who gave me my very own second chance to love, more happiness than I could have believed possible, and healed three broken hearts in the process. I swear I can't love you any more than I already do and the next day proves me wrong.

In Memoriam

To my forever friend, Linda Wilson, whose skills, talents, and belief in me and my work led to this publication and every book I write. Ours is a relationship forged in the fires of pain, loss, love and laughter. Living without you is very difficult.
To Ron Wilson, my best friend, who got me through the best and more importantly, the worst times in my life with his insight, sense of humor, loyalty, and friendship. He thought I could do anything I've ever wanted to do, and he was right.

Acknowledgment

For Carolyn Gilbreath, her counsel and encouragement made this a better book. She is my Best Friend Forever and Beta reader and co-plotter extraordinaire.
And with great gratitude, I acknowledge Jay Austin, extraordinary Editor in Chief; Debbie Nygaard, super-editor; Martine Jardin. artist; Brigit Vries, Assistant to the Editor in Chief, The Greater Detroit Romance Writers of America; and you, my readers. For Doug Marple, webmaster, who keeps the social media site wheels turning. I'm grateful to you all. Lastly for Rick Nygaard, thanks for being my military guru.

Disclaimer. Any military mistakes herein are mine. Currently COVID-19 is still infecting the United States. The treatments mentioned reflect the ever-changing information available at this time. Hopefully, an effective vaccine will work efficiently.

CHAPTER ONE: ON THE ROAD AGAIN

Shit! Fuck! Just when I finally get a chance to get my hair done, a much-needed manicure, and a pedicure, and what happens? Call to Duty! Report to base. Dawn Winters's—make that Second Lieutenant Dawn Winters of the Great State of Tennessee's National Guard—cell phone pinged. It was a text issuing marching orders just as she arrived at Shears Salon, recently re-opened after the Stay Home, Stay Safe order expired.

Off duty, she was a nurse. Things were heating up with a new virus spreading throughout the community like the Chimney Two Wildfire of 2016. Now, she could no longer take the time for grooming. While not a call to battle, she and other medical and military people like her were called to action just as seriously as if they were being deployed for wartime. Today they were fighting another kind of war—the global COVID-19 pandemic.

She had barely pulled into the much-coveted parking spot at Shears Salon with her windows down to breathe the crisp spring Smyrna, Tennessee air. Suddenly, the god-awful screech of metal meeting metal caused her stomach to pitch like a skiff in a storm. Her Volkswagen bug had obviously hit another vehicle.

She smacked her forehead into the steering wheel in frustration, yelling, "Fuck a damn duck!" through the open window. She shoved the gear shift into park and bolted out of her car, ready for combat. There was no time for this. She had places to be, lives to save, a fight to win, and now an accident.

Her body collided with a hunk of an iron-chested giant,

who failed to back up enough to permit her to completely assess the situation. He was literally in her face. Well, he would have been in her face had she been a seven-foot-tall Amazon. As it was, all she saw was a black t-shirt stretched tight across a linebacker — with full gear on — massive chest. A torso that wasn't a featherbed.

His tone, when he spoke, came out in a lazy drawl. "Whoa, Nelly, don't get your panties in a twist, lady. Who taught you to drive? A snowplow driver? And who taught that pretty little mouth to talk so ugly?"

Not one to stay quiet, she didn't miss a beat. "My imaginary seafaring father taught me his colorful language, and my football coach taught me to drive," she ground out. "Did your granny teach you?"

The cad took her by the shoulders and moved her backward, providing much-needed space and relief from those rock-hard abs and hard chest. "How 'bout we take a look-see and figure out how much you owe me for ramming that red M&M into my truck?"

"You mean tank, don't you? That's no truck." The thing rested on huge wheels. "Is it legal to even drive that thing on the streets? That's a King Kong of a vehicle. And I think you crushed my bug. *You* owe *me, mister.*"

The jerk met her rants with a loud guffaw. "Little spitfire, aren't ya?"

She fumed and blew the hair that had fallen from her messy top bun out of her eyes. "Don't you patronize me. Give me your insurance info, and let's get this over with. I'm late. I need your phone, so I can sync my data. Be sure to include your insurance company, too."

He handed it to her with a half-grin, steered her backward, and took a long look. "Not even a fender-bender, but I can't say the same for your VW. Why don't you call *your* insurance company, and I'll get you to where you're in such a hurry to go. Name's Drew Sunrise, by the way." He looked at his phone and her contact data. "Dawn is it? But tell me, where in tarnation is the frickin' fire?"

Her temper fumed. "It's Second Lieutenant Winters to you. If you must know, I've been called to active duty. That's why I'm in such a rush."

He whistled at her declaration. "A duty call." He chuckled.

"Beats a booty call," she said and then felt her face flame. *Oh no, I did not just say that out loud, did I?*

He cocked a brow in her direction. "Seriously? I doubt that."

She bit back a smile and nodded. "The power of a syringe in my hand can't be matched."

He winked. "Wanna bet?"

She nodded. "I've seen grown men faint at the sight of a needle."

"Don't you mean gun?"

"Nope. I'm a nurse practitioner with the National Guard. Some folks don't like shots."

"I like 'em, all right. 'Specially if they're Tequila."

Dawn bit back a laugh.

He grew serious. "You're being called in to fight the coronavirus?"

"I am."

"Thank you for your service. That takes guts. Look, it doesn't matter who's at fault here. You have a job to do and no wheels. Let me get you where you need to go. It's only fair, and this mop and fuzz can go a few more days without a trim."

She took a close look at him, and what met her eyes was all but stunning. He was one hot dude. His hair was now being secured into a low dark brown ponytail, while his face wore a kinda sexy stubble on its way to becoming a beard. Chocolate eyes smiled at her, the crowfeet beside them only highlighting his *gotta be* fifty-something years. A quick glance at his ring finger revealed no telling gold band or pale skin from one being recently removed.

Seeing no choice but to take him up on his offer, she shook off her false pride and attitude and followed his advice.

Her bug looked smashed. Its engine hissed, leaked, and smoked. She took photos of the damage to send to the insurance company while noting his truck had nary a scratch. The impact didn't even appear to reach his bumper. She just hoped her claim would be filed as easily as the television ads promised.

She stretched a leg up to climb into his truck when he opened the door. She didn't make it all the way and fell back into him. His hand shot upward, catching her by her butt, guiding her in safely.

Surprisingly, Dawn liked the tingle caused by the heat of his hand on her fanny, but she didn't enjoy the fact that she *liked* it a little *too* much. More than glad for her fit body, she applauded her workouts to an old program, *Buns of Steel*.

She flashed him a smirk. "I bet you thought I was just a pretty face going for a facial."

He laughed. "Well, you are fragile, sugar."

Before she could detonate, he held up his hands in surrender, shut the door, and circled the vehicle.

Once behind the wheel, he elaborated, "Not delicate like a flower, but more like a bomb is fragile. Handle with care and use extreme caution."

She relaxed and retracted her claws, happy she managed to bite her tongue.

"No, not when you flew into me like a bat from hell. I knew for sure, you got grit beneath your mop of curls. Reminds me of a cute black poodle."

She groaned. "Great, just what every woman wants to hear."

He laughed as she gave him the address and pointed out

where he needed to drive.

"What? You don't like poodles?"

"*Cute*. No woman wants to be *cute*."

He glanced at her, his reply cautious. "I was afraid to say *hot*. You being a female Second Lieutenant and all."

She agreed. "Yeah, dems fightin' words for sure."

He eyed her carefully. "You a libber?"

She stared at him. "A libber? What the hell is that?"

"A Woman's Liberation Movement uh . . . woman . . . Er . . . person."

She laughed, and her voice rose an octave. "Women's Lib? Holy cow. That's an old one. How old are you anyway?"

"Old enough." He slid a glance in her direction. "You don't sound like you're from here."

She smiled for the first time since literally bumping into him. "I'm not. What gave me away?"

"Your accent."

She gave a big belly laugh." Really? My accent? Mr. Southern Dude."

He tried again. "You're not from here. Obviously. Where y'all from?"

"Sunny California."

He slapped his forehead. "That's a long sight from here."

"I'm visiting my friend, Marie, and using my twin sister's place until I decide where I might settle next." She looked at him sideways. "You live here?"

"Nope. Live about three hours east. Just here meeting with a consultant, and it's back home to Molly I go."

"Turn here." *Who's Molly? He wears no ring. Why do I care? I'm not gonna marry him! For all I know, Molly is his pet gerbil. Or goldfish. I don't think I'd give him custody of my cactus. Maybe Molly's a dog . . . a basset hound. That sounds about right.*

He smiled. "I got it. GPS." *You have reached your destination* sounded from the dashboard. "See?"

She thanked him as she moved to get out, declaring she

could fend for herself and get a ride.

"Look, I got nuthin' else goin' on. You have no wheels. How about I drive you to the base?" He looked contrite.

"I can take an Uber." *He's trying to make amends. Give him a chance. He's hardly a serial killer.* "Look, you don't owe me anything. All I need to do is grab my go bag."

"That's a thing? Really."

She winked. "It is, and it's ready. I'll just be a second."

When she accepted his help out of the truck, she couldn't miss the jolt of electricity igniting her insides. *Uh-oh.* After she dug out her key. After she unlocked the door. After she donned her fatigues. After she watered her lone cactus. After she grabbed her twin sisters' computer. After she thanked God that she had no kids dependent on her, let alone a spouse to inform. She finally hefted her duffle bag, retrieved an extra facemask, closed the blinds, locked up, and — with a mental kick in her ass — accepted Drew's offer and used his help to get back into the truck.

"Here." She handed him a face mask emblazoned with the American flag.

"What's this?"

"My peace offering. I came off like a bitch on wheels — literally. You're going to need this. Especially since my orders are directly related to the surge in coronavirus numbers."

"Aww. Ain't that sweet. Didn't know you cared."

"Get over yourself. It's just a mask."

He grew serious. "No, it's PPE, and it's already damn hard to get. Thank you."

"That's my line."

"Truce," he said, holding out his hand.

She took it, felt the zap of heat, and replied, "Truce."

Chapter Two: Molly Mae

Dawn arrived on base after assuring Drew she'd take care of herself and in an instant went from no-damsel-in-distress to a warrior. She returned salutes and strode to the Captain's office. Her orders were to deploy with a thirty-six-person platoon and assist with transforming the Sugarlands Lodge in Gatlinburg into a barracks for the soldiers and possibly a field hospital to handle the overflow of COVID cases from the areas' quickly filling hospitals.

Her unit was to be issued PPE supplies and a host of medical equipment, including several ventilators and other therapeutics. She ordered additional testing kits, just to be on the safe side. She reviewed the roster the Captain provided and noted she'd worked with many of them in the past. Several of the guards worked in labs and would be able to process the coronavirus tests. She also noted she was not the only one with a medical background. *The more medics, the better.*

She nodded her approval of the arrangements.

Not all of her unit had arrived yet. She'd have to spend the night at the armory, but that'd give her time to study the supply list and compile whatever else she thought they'd need. The rest of the team would be there the next day, and she'd convene and brief them on their mission. With calm, she dispatched personnel to load the vehicles they'd need.

That evening after chow, she tamed her unruly locks with a handy-dandy pair of shears. She cut her curls as short as possible, leaving enough for a very tight bun. It wasn't the worst haircut ever, but it was close. She chuckled when she thought of Drew and his poodle comments. All she needed was a pert bow. Instead of that, she adjusted her uniform field cap and figured that move would do the trick.

The remainder of the unit arrived at 0500 the next morning. The private first class called the roll, and Dawn briefed her team.

"Our mission is to assist the people of Townsend, Wears Valley, Gatlinburg, Pigeon Forge, and Sevierville in any way possible. To accomplish that, we must be prepared to deploy and provide any and all community needs for transport, food, and supplies to the general population. We will first establish a base barracks at the Sugarlands Lodge in the Great Smoky Mountain National Park. We will use Metcalf Bottoms Parking lot as a staging theater. In addition, we'll be used to potentially create additional field hospitals, as necessary. Carry on."

They formed a convoy and began the three-and-a-half-hour drive to Gatlinburg.

As they drove, she reviewed the mission ahead of her. By her estimation, it was at least a six-fold assignment, give or take. One, purely personal.

She needed a plan to deal with Eve, her twin, who worked at the Sugarlands Lodge. That could be tricky. Their relationship was fraught with the usual twin issues — who's in charge. She was the younger of the two, though only by minutes, but Eve always played that card. Dawn's authority could not be compromised or cluttered with unnecessary complications. *That will be no small feat.* She snapped her fingers. *Got it! I know how I'll enlist her compliance and cooperation.* Mentally she ticked off her tasks. *Neutralize Eve, establish the barracks and staging arena, transport goods, services, and people, establish an overflow field hospital, not to mention provide medical care as necessary.*

Once they reached the Sugarlands Lodge, Dawn ordered

the driver to park in front of the Lodge, and her unit piled out. She marshaled a smaller contingent to accompany her inside. The others she deployed to the staging area to begin recon at Metcalf Picnic Grounds.

Her military uniform included a cap, which shielded her face. *Eve won't recognize me for the few precious seconds I'll need to secure her silence.*

There was something about the seriousness of a military presence that automatically insured silence. Through the windows, Dawn noted a small group standing in the reception area, Eve among them. With those gathered at the Lodge was a tall, somewhat familiar figure, but her attention had become laser-focused on the tasks at hand — and Eve — so she paid him no more attention.

A private rapped on the Lodge door. Then they entered the premises.

Dawn wondered if Eve knew it was her but put the thought aside as she made her official announcement. "I am Second Lieutenant Winters. By executive order of Governor Lee of the great state of Tennessee, the Sugarlands Lodge will hereby be under quarantine due to the coronavirus. All personnel is to prepare to stay under quarantine here. The Lodge will become the barracks for Emergency Response and Preparedness."

She stood at ease while one of her privates listed the details of what was expected during their occupation and handed out forms for the civilians to complete. Another private handed out some of the N95 masks from the supply they had brought along.

A ripple of alarm spread through those gathered, but she was not moved by their reactions. She was in command and had a mission to accomplish. Her word — for the duration — was law.

Trained to be aware of her surroundings, she made a quick visual scan of the civilians inside. A small group surrounded an open-mouthed Eve, including a well-decorated purple-haired teen, a platinum-haired, well-dressed woman about her age, and a silver fox. There was also the mystery mountain of man present, but she gave him scant attention, since he was turned away.

Eve led her and her contingent on a brief tour of the Lodge, including the Banquet Room, where numerous cots were set up six feet apart to maintain social distancing. Her unit was already starting to come in, getting assigned their bunks and setting up their gear.

"From past experience as an emergency relief center, we have these cots and bedding ready, as well as the second floor which has eighteen rooms," Eve explained. "We also have a dozen cabins out back that can house the staff. There are Family Quarters as well, since this is a family run Lodge. Let me know how I can be of further assistance to you."

When they returned to the Great Room, Dawn nodded to the assembly. The mystery man finally turned around to face her, and she tried not to gasp. It was Drew Sunrise, of all people, standing silently among the civilians. *It's a wonder I didn't recognize him. What the hell is he doing here?*

Dawn ignored Drew for the moment. It was time to start getting things organized. She nodded to the private next to her. He proceeded to explain the Stay-at-Home orders and how everyone was expected to conduct themselves during the pandemic. Special emphasis was placed on wearing masks anytime they were outside and maintaining social distancing wherever they went.

She needed to obtain a list of everyone currently present on the premises. They were now considered *occupants* and would remain in isolation with her and her unit until further notice. The forms the private handed to Eve would get Dawn the information she needed to get the site prepared. Her team was charged with securing the Lodge and assisting the neighboring towns of Townsend, Wears Valley, and Gatlinburg during this pandemic.

When the private completed his explanations, Eve frowned. "I see." She turned to the others in the room. "Well, everyone, you heard the man. Beau and, uh, family, please fill out the paperwork, get your possessions together, and let's get crackin'."

Dawn crossed her fingers when Eve sent a frown in her direction — the twin signature signal she and Eve had devised — meaning *keep quiet, I'll fill you in later.* Eve's brow rose, but Dawn nodded and complied. Eve gave her a wink, which she prayed no one else noticed. With a quick glance at the others, it appeared no one had, since they were all standing there frozen and looking confused. She was relieved her secret was safe for the moment. With Eve's help, the paperwork was distributed to everyone present.

Dawn collected the completed forms and turned to Eve. "I need to secure a quiet space where I can work. Is there somewhere I can set up as my office?"

Eve pointed to a door behind the counter. "I'm the acting co-COO here. You can use our office."

When the door closed behind them, Dawn restrained her humor at the situation. "All right. Ms. co-COO is it, eh? I'll look over these forms and let y'all know where your quarters will be."

Eve just stared. "There are cottages out back, as I mentioned. I occupy Mr. McGregor's currently. The other cabins have been cleaned and prepared." She paused for a moment. "Some occupants may be getting groceries, belongings, or prescriptions."

Dawn nodded, looked at forms in her hands, and said, "I'll need a list of Lodge accommodations and cabins. I need to know how many bedrooms each cabin has, which are efficiencies or suites. I'll let you know if you can continue to stay in whozit's cabin."

"Mr. McGregor's," Eve muttered. "I can pull that information up easily enough. My half-sister, Storme, has already prepared a spreadsheet you'll find helpful. She prepared a map of the premises for our guests, which I'll also provide."

A smile tugged at Dawn's lips. "Half-sister, eh?"

Eve nodded. "I'll leave you to it. If you need me . . ."

"I'm sure I can find you."

Eve left the office, and Dawn spent some time reviewing the spreadsheet Eve had supplied. When she returned to the lobby, some of the civilians had their heads bent over clipboards, filling out the additional forms required for essential personnel of the Lodge. She located Drew, standing off to the side, and strode over to him.

In low tones, she asked, "What the hell are you doing here? You understand you're now under quarantine, don't you?"

Eve obviously noticed her interaction with Drew and came over to join them.

"Drew, have you met Second Lieutenant Winters? It seems like you know each other."

"You could say we've run into each other in the recent past."

Dawn bit back a laugh. *He's witty.*

"Drew is Beau Jobs' Communications partner. He's here helping get the Lodge up to speed, since we're essentially not hooked up to the outside world. We're known for our rustic way of life, but with our emergency center responsibilities, we've got a massive job to do so we can be useful during the pandemic."

Dawn cocked her brow. "Is that so? Interesting. Whatever. Please be sure you complete the residency forms." *What are the chances Drew would end up here?*

Drew frowned. "I have Molly to consider."

"Include her on the paperwork then. We'll assign accommodations for the two of you shortly." *Molly Polly Golly. Who the hell is she? And why do I care?* Dawn returned to her unit and began assigning bunks in Banquet Room One. She noticed Eve's head bent over her cell, obviously texting. *She's probably sent out some kind of S.O.S. knowing her.*

Drew saw Sunny and Storme when they arrived at the front of the Lodge. He noticed them holding an intense conversation with Eve and wondered what was up. He prayed they weren't conspiring against Dawn's authority.

The three girls, Sunny, Storme, and Eve, returned to the Great Room in the Lodge. Drew, acting as casual as he could, trailed behind them. Then the silence was broken by the sound of boots hitting the floor. The private with the clipboard had returned, as had Dawn.

"I see y'all are ready to settle into your quarters." Dawn flashed a half-smile and cleared her throat, then began to assign accommodations. "The Baby Bear Cabin is assigned to Jesse and Sunny Days. Craig and Storme Knight will occupy The Three Bears Cabin, not the family rooms herein. John and Marsha Weathers will use Little Old Woman's Cabin while Deborah and Jake Jobs will take Jump Over the Moon Cabin with Beau Jobs. Millie and Hank will be assigned to The Bakers Cabin."

Drew almost laughed out loud when a heated discussion resulted from Beau being assigned to stay with his ex-wife. Beau was not only his boss but also a friend, so he was aware that Beau staying with Deborah would not work out well. He noticed Beau's expression light up when Dawn finally assigned him to stay in a cabin with Eve. *I wonder if something is brewing there.*

Deborah continued to complain until Dawn spoke up. "You and your son are welcome to use an army tent. They're primitive but comfortable. The two of you can quarter in the Elkmont Campground if you prefer. The restroom facilities are a short walk away."

Deborah sighed. "Jump Over the Moon Cabin it is."

Dawn turned back to her roster and said, "Lastly, Drew and Molly Sunrise will be assigned to Mother Hubbard's Cabin."

Chapter Three: Chances Are

Drew had been stunned, to say the least, when he first saw Dawn march into the Lodge. *Who would have thunk it? What were the chances Dawn's military mission would end exactly where I'm working? Nobody would believe it. But here it is. Our paths crossed again. I'd never have made that bet had I been asked to wager on it.*

The activity at the Lodge had simmered down, and Drew thanked his lucky stars that he hadn't messed with Dawn when they'd first met. She was fierce, not fragile in any way, much like his sister, Marianne.

Ever since Marianne was deployed with the army, Drew held temporary guardianship of her daughter, Molly. He took the role seriously. He loved his niece to pieces. His sister's rat-bastard boyfriend had abandoned Marianne upon discovering she was pregnant. Drew had stepped in to help raise Molly and provide stability for them both. He was grateful Molly would be here where he could keep her safe during the pandemic. He let out a huge sigh of relief.

He got a chuckle out of the cabin's nursery rhyme names. Molly would get a kick out of it when she left St. Mary's Resident Academy for Catholic Young Women for Spring Break. The plans were she'd spend the break with him. He'd texted the Lodge address to the Patrick's, her roommate's parents, to confirm his location change. He doubted it'd pose a problem, and if it did, he'd figure it out.

Drew had already been to his hilltop home on Skyway Drive and gathered his effects. He was back at the Lodge and heading to his cabin when he saw Dawn striding down the path.

"Where ya goin', Second Lieutenant?"

Dawn's head snapped up, and her blue eyes widened in surprise when she looked up at him. "I was thinkin' of lighting the campfire. Gotta give folks something to do before their world shuts down. And that way, I can make sure folks are shown proper social distancing. This is our brave new world nowadays, after all."

It was his turn to be surprised. "We can still do that, have a campfire?"

Her tone held fatigue. "If folks follow the rules, yes. And if we follow fire-wise regulations. Most are still busy settling in, so I thought I'd snag a few minutes of peace and quiet. We're going to be busy for the next several weeks. Wanna join me?"

They walked over and sat cattycorner from each other. Close but not too close.

Dawn threw him a look. "I can't believe we both ended up at the same place! What are the odds?"

He smiled. "I was just having that conversation with myself. How about zero to none?"

She returned his smile. "What do you make of it?"

"Déjà vu?" Then taking a beat, carefully considering his words, he added, "Fate. Must be fate."

She let fly a huge belly laugh.

"Wait a minute. What's so funny? You have something against fate?"

Her tone was wry when she replied, "Let's just say fate and I had words a while back, and I'm no longer a fan."

"What'd fate ever do to you?"

She looked at him through half-closed eyes, as if recalling another time, another place. "For starters, it led me to marry Dr. River Winters, the icy cold son of a bitch. I pushed my dreams aside, put off having children, getting my degree so he could become — a stone-cold surgeon. One who left me for" — she made air quotes — "a *study buddy.* Now, they have two kids. And I have none."

His sudden concern for Dawn surprised him, but he held it back. "Ouch."

She sat up straight. "Sorry 'bout that."

He forced a smile. "I'm not."

She threw him a half-smile. "Still, I don't like pity parties. I usually don't bore people with them."

"Your life's not boring. Sounds fascinating to me. If you were still married, our paths wouldn't have crossed." He leaned into her space, kissed his fingertips, then outlined her lips through the facemask. "Think about that. Paths cross for a reason."

"Ours crossed by accident. Nothing more, nothing less."

He winked. "So you say. I don't believe in accidents. I believe things happen for a reason, for the best, and the best is yet to come. You'll see. People meet because they're meant to."

She stared at him and murmured, "With all due respect . . . Yeah, sure."

"Time will tell. Fate brought me good things. It brought me Molly." He left her then and headed to his cabin to settle in.

Absently, Dawn traced her lips and watched the bonfire ebb but not die. *The mysterious Molly again.* She heard a noise and startled. Looking up, she recognized one of her new half-sisters.

"Relax, it's just me. Storme Knight. What's got you out here all alone with a dreamy look on your face? Was it that hot guy, Drew Sunrise? I saw him just a minute ago with the same dazed look on his face."

"Wh-what? No! Just taking a breather, that's all."

Storme didn't miss a beat. She winked. "Uh-huh. Sure you are. Just saying."

"I thought I'd enjoy the fire . . ." *Maybe I can distract Storme. It'd be like stopping a tornado but worth a try.* Her focus landed on Storme's ring. "That's a cool wedding set. Looks like Holly."

Storme's expression turned dreamy. "My husband gave me a kitten for Christmas named Holly. The ring was attached to her collar. He claimed holly was *mountain mistletoe.* He got many a kiss claiming that." She waved her hands like a fan cooling herself. "You married? Any kids?"

"No, and sadly, no again. Divorced. Too old for kids now, and a good thing, since I'm single. You?"

Storme sighed. "Not for lack of trying. We've only been married a little while, but I thought we'd conceive right away, but nooo."

Dawn could sympathize. "How long have y'all been trying?"

"Since we were married."

"When was that?"

"Last Christmas."

"It's only March."

Storme scrunched her brows. "I know, right?"

Dawn chuckled. "You are a goof."

"Am not."

"Are too." *Yup, we're half-sisters, all right.* "Doesn't look like anybody's planned on joining us for the fire. I guess I should put it out."

"Don't bother. No worries. Ranger Luke Scraper, my brother-in-law, is on his way to do just that."

"Your brother-in-law? Is everyone out here related?"

"Just about." Storme smiled. "Or kissin' kin." She gave a brief nod, then headed off to wherever she had come from.

Dawn waited for Luke, since she didn't want to leave the fire unattended. When he got there, she assisted him with dousing the flames, then left for her quarters.

She was proud of herself for COVID-cuffing Eve and Beau. She'd noticed the sparks flying . . . everyone did. Besides, Eve had written plenty about Beau in her last email. Now, Eve owed her one, and she couldn't bitch about it, because Cupid wanted what Cupid wanted. *Any fool could see I merely helped her reach her objective.*

As she made her way back to her quarters, she tossed the idea of family around again. Her thoughts tumbled like clothes in a dryer, showing a piece here, a whimsy there. What if she did seek out her father after all? He was here. What if she found he wasn't a bad guy? It wasn't his fault he had been MIA in her life. Poor guy hadn't even known she and Eve existed. No clue at all. Still, it was Eve who'd found the courage to go after what she wanted. Roots. The question was, did Dawn? Would she regret it if she didn't take the opportunity to connect? *Hmm, when ya ask for a bike, ya better pedal. I could have a family — weirdly made, granted — but still a family, after all, with a set of parents, sisters, and nieces and nephews. A bike would allow her to pedal away if things didn't pan out . . . Hold on a minute. You, girl, are no coward. You are a warrior, so go forth and conquer.*

She noticed a light on in the back of the Lodge and decided to investigate. *What the hell?*

CHAPTER FOUR: MEET ME AT MIDNIGHT, EVE

Dawn entered the Lodge's kitchen to find her twin, humming the classic melody from Eric Carmen, *All By Myself*. Eve appeared to be baking cupcakes. *At this hour? She must be pissed about something. She's mixing up a storm.*

"You're baking? Now?"

Eve jumped and placed a hand over her heart. "You scared the bejesus out of me! Baking helps me sleep when my thoughts get . . . uh . . . hungry."

Dawn grinned. "You mean your belly."

Eve's laugh confirmed it.

"You used to bake when you got mad."

"Same difference. I guess the word is *hangry*."

Dawn removed her cap, unbound and shook out her short curly locks, and gave Eve a crushing hug. She picked up a spatula, used it as a mic, and sang the chorus of the song Eve had been humming.

Eve glared at her. "Spill."

Dawn laughed. "What and ruin the fun?"

Eve chuckled. "Why the secrecy?"

"I had to do what I had to do officially first. Morale, keeping up appearances, and all that yadda, yadda, yadda. It was more fun to keep my twin-ship secret so my message wouldn't get lost in the twin thing. You should have seen the look on your face. I shacked you up with your boy toy, didn't I? Some thanks I get. We should be talking about how and why I'm here, ya know."

Eve hooted as she placed the last cupcake tin in the oven. "We will. First things first. Boy toy? That I can get behind. He just told me not to get serious about him, so that's a perfect description of what he is now."

"He did not!"

"He did."

"The cad."

Eve nodded. "He was the epitome of that old adage *when you find yourself in a hole ya just dug for yourself, stop digging.* But he didn't. He dug himself in deeper."

Dawn sighed. "Men. Can't live with 'em, can't shoot 'em."

Eve laughed. "It's time for you to meet the other set of us. How about I text Sunny and Storme to join us at the fire pit to talk or bond? How's tomorrow night sound?"

Dawn shook her hand in a so-so gesture. "Cum se, cum saw. Just so you know, I already met Storme the first night I was here. Doesn't matter to me. Just as long as we social distance. Six feet away and all that."

Eve nodded. "Can do."

"So I'm gonna get to meet your — our — half-sisters?

"Uh-huh."

Dawn cocked a brow and responded in a dry tone. "I can hardly wait."

At long last, Dawn climbed the stairs to her room to get some shuteye. Once inside, she noticed a tent placard on the mantelpiece. She picked it up and read about Mountain Magic.

According to words of lore
In days of yore,
Those who pass through this cabin door
Will find lasting love evermore.
Tis love y'all find

Of the forever kind
Two hearts resting here, for all time, bind.
So mote it be as y'all see.

Dawn snorted as she laughed. *Hogwash. Looks like the own-*
ers will do anything to draw business. Mountain Magic indeed.

Try as she might, she could not sleep. Then she remembered she had a master key to all the amenities the Lodge had
to offer, and that included the Spa Haus. Maybe a soak in the
hot tub would be just what the doctor ordered. She slipped
into her sweats and shoes and headed out in the night.

Drew was unusually restless. Sunny Days had told him about
the Spa Haus, and it sounded like the perfect ticket. *Maybe a*
stint in the sauna would help me relax.

He found the side door open, and signs inside directed him
to the right spot. He doffed his clothes, and naked as a jaybird,
he poured water on the embers of the sauna, which was still
fired up. He stretched out. *Ahh, heaven. I'm tighter than a drum.*
So wired with worry over Molly and COVID and something else . . .
He preferred not to name that *something.*

Suddenly, he sensed movement in the area, but he wasn't
worried. *Probably another night owl like me.* He felt no compel-
ling need to find out who it was — *as long as it isn't a wild critter.*
He much preferred to live and let live.

The minutes ticked by, and he finally felt ready for bed.
Before he took off, curiosity got the better of him, and he
peeked through the louvered door. His heart stopped. Just
stood still in his chest. *Am I having a heart attack? Did I die and*
go to heaven? What a vision.

By faint candlelight, he saw the most incredible sight of his
life. A butt-naked female, looking like a goddess, stepped into
the Jacuzzi. It was Dawn in the buff, and buff she was. Fit and
firm, but he'd wager soft in all the right places. Her silhouette

shone in the light. His gaze traveled the sweet curves of her full breasts and long legs, then came to rest on the perfect V of her kitty, covered with a mass of black curling bush. She was very graceful in her descent into the water. She leaned her head back, and he could see the tension ease and melt off her. No way in hell did he want to break her solitude.

He could imagine the weight of responsibility she must feel. She needed this break. Probably one of the rare opportunities for much-needed R&R for her. Still, lust stirred in his loins, and his rod hardened and rose. *Damn! Down, boy.* In his haste to leave, he tripped over the metal ladle and water bucket, and it crashed to the floor, echoing through the Spa Haus, disrupting and jarring the quiet of the night.

Moments later, the door was kicked open, and a naked warrior stood at the ready, demanding, "Halt! Who goes there? Identify yourself. You have three seconds until I end you."

There stood Dawn, fierce in her naked glory, ready for a fight. Her hands and arms were held in a martial arts position, poised to strike. Her breasts heaved as she made to follow through on her threat.

Drew held his palms out, showing he was unarmed. *Well, my cock is armed and loaded, but outside of that, I have nuthin'.* "Whoa. Hold on. Drew Sunrise present, and as you can clearly see, standing at attention, ma'am, uh, Second Lieutenant. It's only me."

She relaxed and lowered her fists. "What the hell!"

He backed away and tried to assure her. "I meant no harm. Just unwinding in the sauna. Like you, I heard something and . . . uh . . . investigated."

She huffed. "Stop drooling."

"Uh, okay. Kinda hard. Under the circumstances. Some-things are just beyond my control."

A half-smile crossed her lips. "I can see that. You are dismissed, civilian." With that, she turned and walked away.

Drew shook his head. Naked Dawn was a sight to see. *Man she's stacked. Built like a brick shit house. Why do people say that? She's smokin' hot, no shit!* He toweled off, pulled on his pants, and returned to his cabin. He crawled under the handmade quilt, savored the feel of the crisp sheets, and attempted to sleep. He must have succeeded, because soon after, he had a vision.

Drew knew he must be dreaming.

A naked Dawn was wrapping her long legs around him as he all but impaled her with his throbbing cock. His hands were cupping her ass as he stood. Full, very firm, high breasts were smashed against his chest. He moved her back a bit. Using his tongue and hungry lips, he tickled her nipples. When he plunged into her depths, he knew pure bliss.

He woke when an orgasmic cry wrenched from his throat, which would have woken Molly had she been in the cabin.

He needed a cold shower, but he was sure the Spa House was closed for the night. That vision of the naked nymph most assuredly would keep him awake for hours. *Maybe I can fall asleep, and she'll come to me in my dreams again.* He sincerely hoped his dreams would come true. Especially that one. His cock certainly knew what it wanted—Dawn in all her glory.

Dawn went to bed but not to sleep. Her thoughts tumbled like autumn leaves in the November wind. She gritted her teeth. Memories of Drew—his beautiful torso covered in real man hair—was a huge turn on. She was used to Hollywood's washboard abs, but he had them in spades. His tight, firm-looking ass made her drool and her girly parts drip, but what got her the most was the contours and contrasts of skin and sinew. His shoulders were broad and wide, his waist narrow. The V of his pelvic bones was pant-worthy, and her chest heaved with real, honest-to-God panting.

His arms were ripped with muscles. For a man his age, he had a body that wouldn't quit. She was old enough to remember the Burt Reynolds naked centerfold and had been surprised and strangely aroused by the sight of all that male hair.

The manly body Drew had on him looked luscious, with dark hairs that sprouted everywhere in just the right amounts in all the right places. After seeing a *real* naked man who was not waxed and hairless, she was certain she wanted to explore—thoroughly and to her heart's content—each nook, cranny, crack, and valley he had.

As if that wasn't enough, he had sported a full-on erection as they faced each other down in the Spa Haus. *Oh, I was so ready to take him down and then go down on that throbbing — and I'm sure very hard — dick. To feel that baby in my kitty has to happen. It's my mission as a woman to fully engage, reconnoiter, and see what that cock can do. What the hell am I thinking!* She tried to shake off her lust by doing push-ups. *Maybe a serious bout of calisthenics will rout the lout out of my system.*

CHAPTER FIVE: SISTERS TIMES TWO

After a restless night, Dawn woke well before her unit and had already outlined her tasks for the day. The night before, her thoughts had been a tangled mess. How she was able to rise that morning with laser-focus was a trait she had long cultivated. Ahead of her lay a day of commands.

Half of her platoon would distribute food from the warehouses to Wears Valley. Another group would complete the set up here at the Lodge, beginning with food services. Tables would be moved six feet apart, and a buffet line was going to be established — first for troop use, then sanitized for the civilians. Eve would have to deal with the Guard taking over her kitchen. After breakfast, all other meals would be delivered to the civilian cabins using KP staff.

Others from her unit would administer the coronavirus swab tests. Testing had already been completed by the National Guards members, or they could not accept the assignment.

Dawn took a deep breath. There was enough to do all right.

She called Eve and outlined what she needed to know about preparing Millie, the Lodge cook. She wasn't surprised to hear Eve intended to enlist the help of Skye Scraper, eldest of the sisters — well, if no one counted her and Eve, that is.

"That may take some doing," Eve said. "Is there any way we can start that process tomorrow? I bet if you took a deep breath through your nose, you'd find she's already begun cooking breakfast. Can you let her do her part for the National Guard — just for today? She's very possessive of her kitchen, especially since it was designed to fit her specifications with the latest gizmos. Give Skye and me a shot after she does the first meal."

Dawn thought a moment, then recalled sometimes discretion was the better part of valor. Besides, she didn't really want to deal with Millie either. "Just for today."

She entered the kitchen to find Millie bustling about her kitchen alongside a serious mid-thirty something private assigned to KP. Millie sounded like a fishwife as she argued with said private. Somewhere along the line, Millie had fashioned her own PPE and wore her mask without complaint.

Millie lectured and fussed. "Let's get one thing straight, Private Whippersnapper, and the rest of your take-over crew asses. This is *my* kitchen. You can *assist* me, but don't think I'm turning my state-of-the-art kitchen over to you or anyone else. This is still the United States of America, and don't you forget it. You can be chief bottle washer and soup cook."

Dawn was pleased with the patience, endurance, professionalism, and tact that the private displayed. All he let show was a quick half-smile at her malapropism for sous chef.

"Yes, ma'am." He winked. "But we have to make it look like *I* assigned *you* to take control. Orders are orders, but together we can pull this off."

Millie hmphed in reply and had him scramble eggs and make the toast after she began preparing flapjacks. She added hickory-smoked bacon to the grill while she flipped pancakes in turn. Then she directed the other assigned KP privates to set up the buffet line. At zero five hundred, all soldiers were ready to rise, shine, and eat.

Millie handed the private what looked to be handmade earthen pottery plates.

Millie would not have any argument. "These soldiers will eat off the best we have to offer as my gesture of thanks for their service. I know what y'all are riskin' out there.

Coronavirus is as much an enemy as any other."

Without missing a beat, the private smiled his thanks and set up the crockery. Once the Guard personnel finished eating, the civilians had started making their way to the Lodge, surely drawn by the delicious scent of farm fresh eggs and bacon.

Dawn had decided not to intervene in the kitchen. Still, seeing the line of people, she was determined to increase the KP team to establish meal deliveries to the guest cabins to reduce the spread of the virus.

When she saw the civilians, she made her announcement clear, speaking with authority. "I see y'all came here to eat, and you have your masks on. We have set tables 6 feet apart for your safety. Cabin families may eat together. Starting with lunch today, however, your meals will be delivered to your cabins. After you finish eating, please report to the . . . what's that called? Shopping area?"

"Boutique Space," Another half-sister was quick to correct. "Sunny Days, sir, uh, ma'am."

Dawn raised a brow. "Call me Second Lieutenant."

Sunny looked uneasy and unsure how to respond, despite having just been told. "Yes, ma'am, er, sorry, Second Lieutenant."

Dawn struggled not to smile as she found herself liking Sunny. She reminded her of herself. *Sunny is a bit of a live wire. Bet she could be a heap of fun.* But Dawn had no time for fun right now.

"Everyone will report to the Boutique Space when summoned to discuss their meals. We'll do this cabin by cabin. Also . . . From this moment forward, please, limit yourselves to groupings under ten people, and that's outside. No inside visitors." She noticed a look of concern on the teenager with the tats and piercings. "If you are closely related, you may visit, but must maintain social distance."

Dawn had a full day ahead of her, marshaling her forces against the invisible enemy.

After dinner, Dawn received a text from Eve.

Meet me at the bonfire as soon as it gets dark.

Dawn wondered what her sister was up to. Was she trying to set her up?

Dawn texted her reply.

K

Then she quickly texted another.

Just you n me?

Perhaps.

R u setting me up with Drew?

Who, me?

Don't Even.

She got an emoji of a pineapple in response. *What the hell! What was that supposed to mean?*

She texted her reply with a turnip. *Let her figure that out.*

Dawn put her finger to her forehead, shook her head, then texted Eve again.

Can I borrow some leggings and a top? I don't have any civvies.

Affirmative. But leave my electric blue sweater alone.

After sunset, Dawn lit a bonfire in the fire pit, smiling because she was wearing Eve's coveted blue sweater. The group sat the required six feet apart as Eve introduced Dawn to her half-sisters, Storme and Sunny.

Dawn teased. "By Gawd. We all *do* look alike!"

Eve pointed at her. "This is my twin, Dawn."

Together Storme and Sunny squealed and jumped up and down.

"The first time we met was around another bonfire." Storm nodded. "It's great to officially meet you now. Who knows when or if that would have happened without the coronavirus?"

"The stupid virus is separating folks," Sunny squealed, "but it *united* us." She made a rude gesture with an arm pump. "Take that COVID!"

Dawn scowled at Eve.

Eve huffed. "Settle your feathers, sista. I got your secret signal and figured it was better to wait a bit before we all met. Did want to rattle your military authority."

Dawn nodded and looked at Storme and Sunny. "I thought Mom and Eve were pulling my leg. Like I have a father I can actually meet. And, uh, sisters. We have to be family, after all! Go figure."

Eve grinned. "Told ya so. Poor John. Poor Marsha. It was huge shock. On top of that, John keeled over when he saw me. We all thought he'd had a heart attack. Seems like you and I go back to Woodstock."

Dawn thought about that for a moment. "Well, we knew about Woodstock, but she never said anything about John . . ."

"Mom got around. She probably didn't know his name, the way I heard it. I used a genealogy kit thing . . ."

Dawn smirked. "Inquiring minds want to know. But wow! Genetics got us good." She rubbed her two hands together. "Is there alcohol? Let's get this party started."

"They have this thing down here called moonshine," Eve said. "I don't think it can legally be classified as liquor, but it packs a wicked punch. Try some." She poured some into a convenient large red plastic cup.

Dawn was thunderstruck by their remarkable resemblance to each other as she sipped her moonshine.

Dawn was curious. "You two ever play *Dynamic Duo*?"

Sunny nodded and looked like she understood. "We called it *Twin Switch*."

Storme choked on her moonshine and sputtered. "Too bad you never played by the rules."

"Did too."

"Did not."

Dawn laughed, "Now, I know beyond any doubt we are sisters! We go back and forth just like that, too."

Eve teased. "Do not."

"Do too," Dawn chimed on cue. She winked. "Very mature."

"I'll drink to that," Storme said, pouring another round, then looked at Eve. "Was Dawn a pain in the behind?"

"Oh yeah! From day one."

"Tell me about it," Storme said. "For me, it began at birth. Sunny was a pain from the get-go."

"Wa—"

"Shut up," Storme and Eve said together.

"Let me tell you a story . . ." Eve began. "I was going down an escalator at the mall. I looked across and saw my twin sister! I got excited and yelled, *Hey Sis*, waving for her attention. Turns out I was waving to myself in a mirror."

Dawn countered. "Cuz, you're the mirror image of me, so that doesn't hold weight."

"Does too."

"Does not."

Eve steamed." You're just the rough draft."

"No, you are."

Sunny laughed. "If Skye were here now, she'd say, *Knock it off*."

"What I am," Eve thundered, "is God's way of saying *by one, get one free*."

Storme looked at her and Eve. "We had hand signals."

"So did we!" Eve said.

To demonstrate, they all crossed their fingers. Dawn laughed at incredulous faces when they all used the *same* hand signal.

"What's yours mean?" Eve asked.

Storme spoke first. *"You and me. We got this."*

Dawn came back with, "Ours means *play along, be quiet, I will fill you in later.* I used it when I arrived here yesterday so Eve wouldn't get everyone focused on the twin thingy."

Sunny laughed so hard she choked on her apple moonshine. "My best caper—the one I got in the most trouble over—was when I went to the Prom with Storme's date. Twin Switch, ya know?"

Dawn and Eve squealed in unison, horror-stricken. "You did not!"

Storme growled." Oh, yes, she did."

Eve laughed. "I can top that one. My boyfriend tried to show Dawn this weird-ass mole on his butt cheek. This was before Dawn became a nurse practitioner. See, both of us were easily grossed out, so he thought it was just me being squeamish. Unfortunately, Mom and I walked in on him chasing the wrong sister around the kitchen with half of his butt hanging out as he tried to get her to look at it. Dawn was screaming, *Eew, get away! Pervert."*

They all roared with laughter.

Sunny couldn't speak, but Storme could. "What happened next?"

"He just turned around and left. We never saw or heard from him again, thank God."

Dawn wagged her finger at Eve. "That was not the worst thing you did. She gave me a black eye, tore my best t-shirt to rags, and knocked my tooth out."

In unison, Storme and Sunny shouted, "She didn't!"

Dawn nodded. "She did. Admit it, Eve."

"In my defense, the tooth was loose. Just a baby one." Eve pointed to her chest. "It was my t-shirt to begin with. She swiped from moi. Plus, we were panhandling."

Sunny swallowed. "Panhandling? What kind of childhood did you have?"

Eve answered. "A very unconventional one. We lived in a commune. In the early seventies. In California. The family we belonged to was a cooperative."

Storme sobered, and in a serious tone, said, "Interesting. A commune. With daisy chains and naked romps through sunflower fields?"

Eve groaned. "You ever try romping through a field filled with sunflowers and shit? It's mucky, scratchy, and not fun."

Dawn added, "On top of that pitiful caper, Eve made me wear a wilted daisy wreath."

Eve inhaled and puffed out her chest. "To successfully panhandle, you had to look pathetic. You brought in the most money until your shiner faded and your permanent tooth grew."

"Brat!" Dawn huffed, then she thought a bit. "I did deal a payback, though."

Sunny's face lit with curiosity. "Do tell."

"I came up with *Operation Find Father* and let Eve reconnoiter the scene first. I wasn't going into that minefield."

Eve crowed. "Maybe it was a bit overkill, but look how it turned out. We found a whole family. She's always coming up with operation this-n-that."

"That's a whole 'nother other," Dawn returned.

Storme looked at Eve. "Remind you of anyone?"

"Sunny! She makes everything a mission."

Dawn looked at the sisters. "But I have to admit. We are *real* sisters, after all is said and done. This little tête-à-tête proves it if nothing else. I mean, *look* at us! We even act and think the same!"

A big broad smile crossed Eve's face. "Told ya."

"God help us." Storme refilled their mugs with moonshine and frowned. "This is the last of it. Drink up and make the most of it."

"Welcome to the family," Storme, Sunny, and Eve

chorused.

Dawn raised her cup in toast and gulped the last swallow. "It's late. I need to turn in. This is too cray-cray for me."

"Beware that you don't scare the Ghost Stag," Sunny cautioned.

Dawn sent her a look that said *get real*. "I'm not falling for that any more than I fell for that mountain magic bull."

"Forgive her," Eve said. "She doesn't know what she's talking about. No worries. I'll fill her in."

Sunny and Storme left for their respective cabins.

Eve stayed for a bit as Dawn was dousing the bonfire.

"The folks around here swear it's true. That mountain magic is a real thing, according to the locals." Eve shrugged.

Dawn snorted. "Hogwash."

"It's supposed to be about meeting or finding your soulmate," Eve said. "The point is, did you meet anyone by accident? Turn up in the same place? Cross paths along the line?"

Dawn laughed. "Baloney with bullshit on top. I could never be serious about any man ever again. Not after River. And Drew? Not my type."

"Time will tell."

Dawn shifted her weight and struggled for control. She muttered, "Y'all sound like Drew."

"Mark my words. It could happen. Everyone saw you two making googly eyes at each other."

"Did not."

Eve winked. "Did so." She wiggled her fingers to wave buh-bye.

Chapter Six: Daddy-O

After breakfast, Dawn ordered the testing stations to be set up. The Guard had established a lab in Sevierville where the test samples could be sent. Results would take a few days. She crossed her fingers and prayed they wouldn't have any cases — at least not on the premises. If worst came to worst, she did have reagents here for emergency testing, but she wanted to save them just in case, use those as a backup. Besides, she had taken steps to keep COVID at bay. *No one could get sick with all my precautions in place, right?*

The CDC, Centers for Disease Control and Prevention, had prepared a list of questions each testee had to answer. Two stations were tasked to ask the variety of CDC questions. Two other stations took temperatures, and the last two administered the swab test. Dawn watched and listened to see how this rotation operated.

She overheard one of her unit asking the series of CDC questions. "Any fever? Any cough? Loss of Taste? Can you smell okay? How's the appetite? Chills? Body ache? Change in color of toes? Have you worn a mask? Where have you been recently? Have you been exposed to anyone with COVID-19? Feeling any fatigue?

That seemed to go well. She approached the next staging area. They took each person's temperature and recorded it on a centralized spreadsheet on their tablets. She moved on and observed the swabbing process. She decided to combine the swabbing and the temperature check, as that went the quickest. She didn't want a backlog. She could use the extra team to relieve the other two, so no one got worn out and made a mistake.

Testing began with the Lodge staff, which included Eve, the Weathers' family, and Millie. Beau Jobs and his family, Drew Sunrise, and others followed next. There were six stations. Dawn coordinated with the six stations and later ran a line herself. She checked Eve's data, concerned about her cough.

"Buck up, Buttercup. Take one for the team." Dawn placed the test swab deep within Eve's nostril.

Eve had closed her eyes and opened them in shock when the swab entered her nostril. Dawn handed the swab to another team member, who took it, capped, sealed, and labeled it with Eve's data. Dawn then added a red tag to flag it for immediate analysis.

The next person in line followed the same procedure. Dawn was beginning to tire out when she looked up to find a salt and pepper long-haired woman wearing a full gypsy skirt, bangle bracelets, tie-dye matching top with a fringed vest.

"Lordy, you sure are family. Y'all must be Dawn. Mighty good to finally meetcha. Wrong circumstance, though. I'm your stepmom, Marsha Weathers." She flashed a smile. "And back there? That handsome son of a gun? That's John, your pa."

Dawn was so surprised she nearly dropped the precious swab. She steadied her gloved hands and returned the greeting, stuttering out a hello.

Once Marsha stepped away, Dawn took a deep breath, faced her father, and administered the test. Unlike Eve, he didn't flinch. Perhaps he felt as awkward as she did. Or maybe he had been subjected to worse in his life. In any case, he took it like the mountain bred man he was.

"John Weathers, I presume? I'm Second Lieutenant Dawn

Winters, Eve's twin. Fancy meeting y'all here."

He smiled big and broad and put his hand over his heart as if to quiet it.

Dawn had heard of his initial reaction to Eve and hoped he didn't have another shock.

"Y'all okay?" She asked, peering closely at him.

John looked pale and tired. His eyes did not sparkle, nor was there light shining therein. "I just need to sit a spell, if y'all don't mind none."

"Not at all." She pulled a folding chair over, bade him to sit, and checked his pulse. She waited until it evened out and then listened to his heart.

The very heart that was in the body of the man who fathered her. It was unreal.

Meeting her sisters was one thing, but she wasn't prepared for John somehow. She had pushed this moment aside in her mind, hadn't let herself dwell on the reality of him. Yet seeing him in the flesh, well, it was clear by his blue eyes and curly black hair they were from the same bolt of cloth. She had to work hard not to shake.

Dawn didn't want to hurt him, but she was worried for some reason. She checked his vitals and then pulled up the previous station's notes. When asked the questions on the CDC checklist, he had admitted to feeling tired. She called a private over to seal and label his test. She added a sticky red tab to flag and prioritize the sample. COVID-19 hit the elderly particularly hard, and though he looked sturdy and fit, her gut warned her.

A few minutes before the scheduled lunch, Dawn turned her post over to the others and took a break. She didn't want to think, didn't want to feel, but did so anyway. This was her family. *The family I always wanted, and they might be sick with a deadly disease. Including Eve! The suddenly very precious half of my soul.*

Her thought ran a race with her fears, and her fears were winning the battle. She needed to split, and fast. *Retreat was never in my vocabulary, but I have to get out of here.*

She was in charge, and things were well underway. Operation Testing was working with military precision, but Dawn herself, not so much. She needed to do something. But what? Then she heard the old triangle sound announcing lunch. It signaled the residents to return to their cabins, provided their test was completed. Their lunches would be delivered to their respective cabins by the KP team.

Dawn went straight to the mess hall — scratch that — dining room buffet, picked up her lunch, and went out to sit by the stream to eat it. Doffing her boots and socks, she shed her coat, leaving her in an olive-green fatigue t-shirt. She rolled up her pants to her calves, then gingerly holding her box lunch, she carefully crossed the rock-lined path. She found a large gray-back boulder where she could try to settle her jumbled thought while dangling her bare feet in the cold mountain water, breathing in the beauty and listening to the bird and stream song. As soon as she perched on a gray-back in the stream, she heard twigs snap and hoped it wasn't a critter waiting to steal her lunch, but it was worst.

It was Drew, who appeared to have stolen not her lunch but a piece of her heart, judging by the pace it now beat out like a mallet on a kettledrum, hard, fast, unrelenting. *Who knew Drew would end up having this kind of effect on me?*

He opened with, "Fancy meeting you here."

"What are you doing here? You're supposed to be in your cabin awaiting lunch."

"I did go there. See?" He held his boxed lunch out. "I saw you practically flying down the path, so I thought I'd check in on you. By the looks of it, you and Eve are twins, and so are Sunny and Storme. It's evident you're related. Kin and all?"

"Yup."

"Not up for any conversation, eh? What's got you so

shaken?"

Surprising herself, she blurted, "I just met my half-sisters last night, my father and stepmother today for the first time ever. And if that's not enough, I'm worried about John's fatigue and Eve's cough."

Drew raised a hand to his brow, clearly listening, and most likely thinking. "Was their temperature normal?"

"Yes, but . . ."

"Deal with facts, not fears, not feeling. Feelings aren't fact. When you know more, you'll do what you have to do."

Dawn furrowed her brow and bit her lower lip. "Hospitalized them? I'll have to isolate them, at the very least."

He nodded. "Probably. You trained for this."

She threw her hands out in frustration. "There is no preparation for a pandemic hitting your other half and family."

He nodded, as if he got it. "Look, you have the rest of the day filled with work, no doubt. Why don't you meet me at the Spa Haus for some skinny-dipping after sunset?"

Despite herself, the suggestion made Dawn laugh. "So we can have a repeat of Operation Watch Drew's sun rise? Not on your life." She juggled the box and wrappers from her lunch as she withdrew her feet from the river and slipped off the gray-back into the shallow river. The cold water soaked her t-shirt, causing her nipples to stand at attention.

Drew struggled to help her but lost his footing when his shoes slipped on the moss. He fell, practically landing on her, but he managed to land so that his long arms straddled her. "Woman, we have to stop meeting like this."

Her mask was soaked. So was his.

Drew pushed them aside as she sputtered her outrage, but it turned into something else when he bent his head and kissed her lips.

Dawn ignited and deepened her kiss, wanting more. More of everything he had to offer. She knew they couldn't stay that way, in the water with him stretched over her. She yearned to grab him and bring his hard body closer to hers, but reality reared its head. She made moves to get up, then splashed the freezing water at him just to even the scales, throw him a little more off-balance in more ways than one.

Drew grinned. "Brrr! Bet that Jacuzzi beats this cold stream, lady. What do you say we dry off in the sauna? You can toss your stuff in the laundry dryer while you dry out thoroughly." He rose and tried to help her regain her balance.

A jolt raced through her when their bodies touched again. *That was no jolt of electricity. It's a whole danged transformer burst. How can one man make me feel so hot when I just got out of a mountain cold river? If this feeling had a color, it'd be Technicolor.* Dawn had had time to drink in the hard lines of his jaw and full curve of a mouth she wanted to sample.

She took off her t-shirt and wrung it out, then stuck it in the cargo pocket of her pants. *Maybe my body heat will dry it.* She crumpled her bra and added it as well. Then she lifted her discarded coat and put it on so she'd look as normal as possible, but not before Drew got an eyeful.

She caught his smile. "Grow up, Sunrise."

Droplets of river water caught the noon sunlight as it dripped down his face and chest, accommodatingly molding his t-shirt to the hills and valleys of his muscles, accentuating each and every one of them.

Drew stripped his wet shirt off, and sunlight dappled the hairs of his chest most attractively. A contrast of light and shadow hinted at the dark wonders at the hollow of his throat, and hidden treasures at the V of his pelvis teased at his pants' low waist.

A half-smile crossed her lips. *Wonder if he got a rise outta that?* She was close to salivating as she watched the interplay of mountain air hitting his ripped muscles. Her fingers itched to romp through the sun-kissed forest on his sculpted torso. She licked her lips.

Dawn took note of each move he made, as if she were a mountain lion studying her prey. *Hubba, hubba, what a mighty fine-lookin' hunk of man.* She wanted to pounce and get herself a piece of that. Oh, yes, she did. Instead, she concentrated on the unyielding fabric of her military coat, not enjoying the unpleasant contact of tender skin on unforgiving material.

She gritted her teeth. *Not much I can do under the circumstances.* The army fabric chaffed her tender breasts. "I'll go in the back entrance, use the fire escape steps to my quarters and meet you at the sauna if I can. But no skinny-dippin' this time."

"Party pooper. Seriously, though. We have to do something about this." His hands gestured to what was between them literally and figuratively. "We're not hormone-driven teenagers. This is basic but real chemistry. We got business to finish."

She almost gasped in surprise. Drew had given voice to what she felt as well.

She quickly covered her shock with professional distance. "I've got work to do, and so do you."

"Think about what I said. Figure out the logistics. That's a military thing, right? Here's your next mission—Operation Monkey Business."

She laughed shakily, then stepped back to put physical distance between them. "You know duty calls and all?"

"You could probably warm up with a booty call." He winked.

She smiled. "Duty calls." *At least he appreciates my girlie parts. No doubt he's right about the heating and warming up.* She turned away and headed back to the Lodge.

When Private Williams found her, she saluted and said, "Ma'am, everyone's been tested. These coronavirus tests are ready to go to the lab. The tagged ones are in front. Do you want me to drive?"

Dawn returned the salute. "No need. I'll do it. I want to check the staging areas, Mountain Heritage Hospital, and the warehouses to see how food and supply distribution is proceeding. I need you to do a cabin sweep, see how the civilians are doing, and I need tents in the Elkmont Campground prepared in case we need them."

Dawn gritted her teeth. The wet t-shirt was uncomfortably soaking through her pocket. Drew was quite right. She was missing out on a nice warm sauna. *Maybe tonight . . . I wonder if his hands could warm me up? For sure a booty call would.* Her thoughts shot back to the night at the fire pit. She had swapped her N95 for a camo-colored cloth mask. Her lips tingled at the memory of his finger, tracing her mouth through the material. Her girlie parts grew moist.

At the end of the grueling day, having completed a myriad of tasks, including driving the test swabs to Sevierville, Dawn was consumed with fatigue. Despite her intentions, and as good as a long soak with a charming champion sounded, she was too beat for the heated Jacuzzi. She arrived at the Lodge after nightfall and ran into Eve while heading to her quarters.

Eve scrutinized her carefully. "You look too pooped to participate in tonight's bonfire, and the twins are nowhere in sight. Their cabins are dark. They must be having their own private party. Killjoys, all of you."

"Maybe not. Maybe they'll show up later, or Beau will." Dawn plopped her cap on Eve's head. "Go as both us of. Wear my cap when you're me and take it off when not."

"Dynamic Duo. I love it, but I think I'll find something somewhere to do. Thanks for the hat."

Dawn chuckled and tossed a dismissive wave over her shoulder, then headed for her bed. "You're dismissed" was the last thing that fell from her lips.

"No," Eve shot back. "You're dismissed."

Dawn caught a glimpse of Eve's mock salute but didn't feel up to taking the bait. She was too bushed to even bother.

In the end, Eve decided to use the Spa Haus. After all, she was co-COO and had a key. She went to the Spa and doffed her clothes but kept Dawn's hat on to keep the bubbles from the water jets from hitting her eyes. She turned on the low purple lights and slipped into the bliss-inducing hot water. She tipped the brim over her eyes after checking her toes to see how her pedicure was faring. Lord only knew when nail salons would open again. She nearly fell asleep to the soothing playlist of Enya songs when a male voice broke her into serenity.

"Aha! There you are. I see you took my advice and changed your mind about skinny-dipping. You know, we've got to stop meeting like this." His penis rose and stood at attention. "You're lookin' good, Dawn."

Eve let out a screech and scrambled to cover herself.

"I've already seen you naked. What's all the fuss about? Like you predicted, Sunrise rose to the occasion and stands at attention for the Second Lieutenant, ma'am."

"At ease, soldier. But I'm Eve. Not Dawn!"

"Why are you naked?"

"I'm not. I'm wearing a hat, and"—Eve pointed to her leg—"a tat." She directed his focus to a tattoo of a small rose on her ankle. "It ought to be obvious as to what I'm doing. Trying to relax."

"Christ on a horse!" Drew scurried into his clothes, grabbing anything he could to cover his man parts. "It might be best not to discuss this with Dawn."

"But we tell each other *everything*. This is going to be heaps of fun. How is it you've seen her naked anyway?"

"Ask Dawn. Apparently, she doesn't tell you everything."

CHAPTER SEVEN: GOOD GOLLY, MISS MOLLY

Dawn was in the vicinity when Molly Sunrise was dropped off at the Lodge. The girl wore a hot pink bandana as a facemask that matched her cap of short hair. She looked to be fifteen years old if she was a day. There was something fragile like a flower—*not* like a bomb—about Molly. Dawn immediately felt drawn to her, as if Molly was a magnet. She looked like a motherless, lost little lamb. She definitely needed an N95 facemask.

"Be sure to exchange that bandana for an N95 mask. What you are wearing is practically worthless." Icy coldness seeped from her lips. "You're not old enough to be married! What in all that's holy is Drew thinking? You're a *girl*, a very young girl, I might add, not a *woman*. Are you here of your own volition? Have you been hurt in any way?"

Molly paled and looked baffled. "Pardon?"

"Are you Mrs. Drew Sunrise?"

"What? Eew! No. I'm his godchild. He's my uncle. I live with him when my mom's deployed. She's military. I'm on Spring Break, and I guess I'm under quarantine like he is. Where is he?"

Dawn tried to hide her surprise. *Oh, good grief! This is Molly? The Molly I've been dreading? I feel like a complete ass. I've been feeling threatened by his niece? A young girl? Holy Moly. Is my face red or what?*

"Looks like you made a mistake," Molly said. "Mistaken identity or sumthin'."

Eve interjected in a wry tone. "There's a lot of that going on around here lately. Last night, Mr. Sunrise thought I was you at the Spa Haus. I was skinny-dipping wearing your hat."

"Cap." Dawn corrected automatically. "Not a hat."

"Whatever." Eve smirked and texted Drew, presumably.

Dawn flushed and turned to leave with as much dignity as she could. She looked over her shoulder and muttered to herself, "Just kill me now. Ya can't fix stupid." *Molly's a kid, not his wife. Geesh.*

As she strode away, Jake, with his purple Mohawk hair, ambled over to the counter. She hoped the two kids wouldn't get up to any shenanigans or do anything young and stupid.

Molly frowned as she watched the military woman march away, still muttering.

"Your uncle is on his way," Eve said. Let's get you properly masked up. Have you been COVID tested?"

Molly looked up in surprise. "Seriously? Tested? Really?" She shook her head no.

Eve nodded. "Prepare yourself. It's not fun. But taking your temperature will be a walk in the park."

A purple-haired teen with a Mohawk arrived just as Eve finished checking her in.

"I'll take her to the testing site," he blurted.

"Oh, Jake, thanks. This is Drew Sunrise's niece, Molly. Molly, this is Beau Jobs' son, Jake. I'll text your uncle to update him. Go ahead."

As Jake led her deep inside the Lodge, where the staging area for administering the test was, he asked, "So, you have any weed with you?"

Molly startled. "No! Why would I?"

"Cuz you're about my age."

Molly was put out. "So, I'm your age, and people like me — with pink hair — automatically do weed? Look at you. Worry about yourself."

She tried to flounce away, but Jake's hand on her forearm stopped her.

"Hey, no, seriously. Dope. I mean, glad you don't use it. I was just trying to keep you out of trouble—just in case. This is a National Park, and you could get seriously busted."

"Who are you? The pot police? I don't do drugs. Do you?"

"Nada. It's not one of my vices." He gestured at his tats, piercing, and Mohawk. "This is as radical as I get. Do you think I should?"

She giggled and shook her head. "No. I go to Saint Mary's Residential Academy for Young Catholic Women, so I think doing drugs is a humongous sin. I could get kicked out of school, and that would be bad. Where would I go?"

Jake cocked his head, slanting a look her way. "Uh, how 'bout home?"

She sighed. "No one is there."

"Say what?"

"My mom's military. When she's deployed, I'm already at St. Mary's. On breaks, I stay with Uncle Drew. It's Spring Break. Uncle Drew is here." She drew a hand in one swoop down her body. "Voila"

"Cool." They reached the testing site. "I'll wait for you."

Molly batted her eyes. "You won't hold my hand or anything?" She closed her eyes and placed her hand over her forehead. "No catching me should I swoon."

"Huh?"

"You know, me being a damsel in distress? For moral support? Talk about Big Brother. Geesh."

He laughed. "Sorry 'bout that. Just didn't want you to get in trouble."

She winked. "I'm just punkin' you."

Jake flushed.

When she got done with her test, she was pleased to see

Jake waiting, leaning against the fireplace.

He saw her and shoved off. "I think your uncle is in the office. You should probably see him first. How'd it go in there?"

She shrugged. "I didn't like it. Gross."

"Later . . ." He paused, spying her uncle heading toward them. He nodded. "Mr. Sunrise. Look who's here to see you."

"Good Golly, Miss Molly!" Drew said, giving her a bear hug and lifting her off her feet. "You are a sight for sore eyes. I see you've met Jake."

She nodded. "He was kind enough to walk me to the testing area." She giggled and fluttered her eyes again. "Like I couldn't find my way, weak little ole me."

Drew threw back his head and laughed. "You didn't?"

Jake's flush deepened, but he threw up his hands. "So, shoot the nice guy. But I'll show you around later . . . if that's all right with you, Molly. And Mr. Sunrise."

They laughed.

He continued. "Show you the ropes of rustic living."

Jake shuffled off as her uncle picked up her duffle bag and led her to their cabin.

"Home sweet home," he said as he dropped her baggage in the charmingly rustic room known as Mother Hubbard's Cabin.

Chapter Eight: Day by Day

Dawn was very busy supervising operations. She had a small squad servicing transport when necessary. It was beginning to look like they might have to build another tent hospital to take some pressure off Mountain Heritage Hospital in Sevierville. Yet another squad was dispatched to staff the Wear Valley-Townsend food bank. She had very little time to think about Drew's naked torso and torrid kisses.

She comforted herself, knowing Drew was putting in long hours installing flat-screen televisions and wiring in the Lodge's cabins and rooms. She limited the communications team to Beau and Drew. Her people could assist if necessary. She left orders regarding that just in case.

From time to time, she spied Jake and Molly's heads together — wearing mandatory masks — as they fished, keeping social distancing. She wouldn't put money on it, but she thought she noticed John and Jake together whittling. That said something about her father. *He seems to be a class act, after all is said and done.*

One day, she saw the kids tubing down the river, their laughter ringing through the hills as they got tossed by the current, rocks, and downed tree limbs. *Only the young would brave those frigid spring waters.*

Dawn was fairly sure she saw the kids fishing with the KP team as well. Millie had insisted on fresh-caught mountain brown trout and catfish, so she had enlisted the KP staff to do the fishing. She had to laugh at how Millie was ensuring her control of the kitchen and marveled at how smooth the endeavor flowed. The fisherfolk were all stationed the mandatory six feet apart. Apparently, the fish were biting, judging by the *hooahs* she heard.

Shortly after the quad's birthday party, she made specific arrangements to test Skye and her quadruplets. Luke and the other rangers considered essential staff were tested at Smoky Mountain Park headquarters.

What would it be like to have a baby? Skye has four! How does she do it? She choked down her feelings about never having what she and Eve deemed a *real* family.

Dawn helped corral the children. She made a game out of it. She took each child one by one and acted as if the swab was a booger snatcher and gave them plastic gold badges saying *Booger Slayer* when they were done. She told the girls the boys nearly cried, then told the boys the girls would never ever, not in a million years, cry. She got through that scenario successfully, praying no one tested positive for the disease.

When it was Skye's turn, Dawn made the children laugh by saying their mama was going to be a crybaby.

"Take this for the team." When Skye flinched, Dawn winced. "Oops, guess that was too deep."

"What did I expect?" Skye ground out. "You are an older version of Sunny. I was going to suggest we meet at the fire pit to bond, but now I'm not so sure."

Dawn shrugged. "Sorry. We're all here, and I just saw Luke pull up. He can watch the kiddos, face time, visit John and Marsha, or throw stones in the river while we social distance. Eve and the gang are here."

Skye's brow raised. "I'm not so sure . . ."

Hearing the ruckus the quads made drew Storme and Sunny like flies on shit. While the quads were occupied with their dad, the Weathers' girls and Eve and Dawn made a socially distanced circle out of the rocking chairs on the front lawn.

Sunny was quick to suggest a game. "Let's play Never

Have I Ever."

Eve was game. "That is a fast way to get to know each other. Raise your hand if you have. Keep it down if you never have. Each person gets to ask one question. We'll see how this works. I'll start. Never Have I Ever made love in the Spa Haus."

Three hands went up. Dawn's stayed down.

Skye was next. "Never Have I Ever been divorced."

Dawn and Sunny's hands went up. Eve, Storme, and Skye's stayed down. That led to a discussion punctuated with many laughs about Sunny's first attempt at *marriages real and fake.*

Sunny looked around and shrugged. "What? Doesn't an annulment count?"

"That's what they called a mountain promise all right," Skye said.

Sunny screeched, "More like a mountain no-no! I'm next." Her expression turned mischievous. "Never Have I Ever hooked a guy with his rod."

Again, laughter enveloped the group. They were slapping their thighs, rocking backward, and tears running down their faces. Dawn nearly choked at the hilarity and explanations of how Storme first *caught* Craig.

Storme grumbled but didn't speak until it was finally her turn. "Never Have I Ever made love in a tent."

Four hands went up.

"Almost did, but Craig blew it," Storme said, laughter bubbling over.

Sunny jumped in with, "That would make it a mountain hot—not."

Skye winked. "That sounded like it could be a mountain hot story if I ever heard one. Never Have I Ever had a Jump the Broom wedding."

"Wasn't there something about mountain holly in that one?" Sunny asked.

Only one hand went up. Skye. She explained how she said *yes* to Luke. "It was just a mountain prequel to all the mountain joy we found." She sighed, looking toward her quads.

Eve screeched. "Oh, oh, I have one."

"You already had a turn," said four voices in unison.

"Did not."

"Did too," Echoed from four throats.

Eve pleaded. "This is a good one, I promise."

They agreed and ceded the floor.

Eve began. "Never Have I Ever played Dynamic Duo in the Spa Haus."

Hoots and hollers greeted that exchange. "Whoa, I bet that would cause a mountain fever."

Dawn laughed with the rest of her sisters, and it felt dammed good. But her thoughts all the while were pinned on Drew and his hot bod.

She finally returned to duty and what seemed like a series of endless tasks. She knew the lab results were ready, and when she checked them using her cellphone, her blood ran cold. Two of her personnel had to be isolated. She swiftly marched to what she considered the war room—a set of rooms set aside for the purpose of strategy on the second floor of the Lodge to keep them isolated from those in the barracks. She gave orders to set up a field hospital in the Ballroom. It had the best ventilation. Hopefully, good, fresh mountain air would help. She crossed her fingers and prayed.

CHAPTER NINE: KEEP ON BELIEVING

Drew was happy Molly had struck up a friendship with Jake, his boss and best friend's son. Maybe Molly would be a good influence. The kid had been through a lot. Their entire family had been rocked by the shock of Kyle's sudden death. For Jake to lose his twin had to have been hell on earth, and Deborah and Beau's divorce hadn't helped.

He was sitting outside Jake and Molly, keeping the social distance. Jake was playing his guitar with Molly as his admiring audience. She seemed to be mesmerized by his soulful music, which touched Drew as well. *Thank God, the kid has an outlet.* Jake abruptly stopped, laid his guitar aside, and strode off. Molly looked baffled. Confusion crossed her features, and her brows furrowed on her forehead.

Drew approached and said, "Let him go. He lost his twin, Kyle, suddenly not too long ago. Jake was there but could do nothing to save him. He's got issues to work out. You didn't do anything wrong. He had to cut and run before he broke."

She looked relieved. *She's got a soft heart. Maybe she can help somehow. Molly's like a magnet. Had been since birth. Drawing everyone she ever met into her orbit. She certainly has me wound around her little finger.*

"Uncle Drew? Tell me about Second Lieutenant Winters. She's so cool. Military like Mom. I'd like to carry on that tradition."

Drew thought about Dawn. *How do you put into words how intriguing she is?* "Well, she comes across all strong and tough, but she cares deeply about those in her charge, and she's . . .

challenging."

Something in his tone must have tipped Molly off. "You like her, don't you?"

"Why do you think so?"

She pumped her fist in triumph. "The look in your eyes, your dreamy tone." She punched him playfully. "You wanna bet she likes you, too."

He winked. "She might."

"See ya later."

"Where are you off to? Stay safe. We're in the wilderness in a pandemic, ya know."

"You worry too much. I'm gonna see if Second Lieutenant Winters is around. Kinda shadow her. See if she likes military life."

Drew watched Molly leave and saw Dawn on the veranda, head bent, looking at her tablet. *Molly couldn't have chosen a better role model. Dawn has it all. Looks, brains, wit, and a wicked sense of humor to boot. Plus, she's sexy as sin.*

John Weathers had joined Molly, and together they approached Dawn. *Ah, the plot thickens. Dawn and her newfound bio dad together. Things could get interesting.*

Dawn spotted John heading her way. *Good grief. Here comes my . . . father.*

He was walking next to Molly, who seemed anxious about something.

Wow. Who'd have thunk I'd ever see him *face-to-face, and now I can see him every day. Wonder what's up with Molly?*

John saluted. "Permission to approach, ma'am."

Automatically, she returned the salute and nodded. *How does he know military-speak? He was a Woodstock hippie into a* make love, not war *mindset. What gives?*

There were shadows in his eyes, and his tone wasn't playful. "I hoped I'd run into y'all . . . spend some time. Looks like

Molly beat me to it."

Dawn quirked a brow at Molly. "Why?"

"I'm looking into career options," Molly said. "My mom's military, and you are, too. So there's obviously a future there. Women can do a lot more than they could in the past, and I'm thinking maybe I should consider it."

"It put me through nursing school and beyond. The National Guard is a good way to find out if military life suits you or not. Plenty of opportunities."

John wagged his finger at Molly. "Don't you be thinkin' the Guard is something to do just to avoid the military draft."

Dawn gaped. *What's going on with John?* "The draft is long gone. Nowadays, it's an all-volunteer profession."

John shook his head, as if clearing away momentary confusion. "Forgive me. Sometimes, I harken back to the past whether I want to or not. I was drafted during the Vietnam War. You can take the boy out of the Army, but you can never get rid of the war that's involved him. What I meant to say was the Guard isn't soft. Basic training is the same for them as anyone else. Folks think they're civilian soldiers, but they're more than weekend warriors."

"Case in point," Dawn affirmed, running a finger down her length. "The Guard helps out during pandemics, floods, natural disasters, riots, and other periods of civil unrest. You could do a lot worse than join. It's a very dynamic and varied field. Are you in the high school ROTC?"

Molly shook her head. "I don't know if Saint Mary's has a chapter, but I'll look into it. Thanks."

Dawn reflected on what John had revealed. "I didn't know you were drafted. I only knew about *Woodstock John*, and even then, that info came late in life."

"Now, that is just another regret," John murmured. His words were broken by a cough that nearly left him breathless.

Dawn stepped closer and whipped out her ever-present

digital thermometer. "You have no fever, but I don't like that cough. Let's go. Molly, you'll excuse us." Then she saluted and said, "We can talk more whenever you can catch me, but right now, I want to check John out. Dismissed."

Molly playfully returned the salute. "Aye, aye, Capitan. Oops . . . or whatever." She flicked a cute finger wave and went toward the stream.

I remember John complaining about fatigue. I'm not happy with Eve's cough, either. When I brought her back a special blend cara-mel-hazelnut coffee with sprinkles — her absolute fav — she didn't rave about the delicious aroma or taste. Another physical sign not boding well for her health.

Dawn had already had to use their field hospital. Two of her peeps were in the infirmary. She steeled herself, gritting her teeth and preparing herself to win this battle. Her attention returned to her father.

John cast his eyes down and then looked up at her half-lidded. He shifted his weight and held his hands out in supplication. "Dawn, I didn't know you and Eve existed. I would have been there somehow, someway, not that I'd have been much good. The war messed with my head, and after Charlie, my fellow medic—"

"Wait." Dawn stood stock still. "You were a medic? Wow. Not only were you military, but in medicine as well." *Like me. Holy cow. Fancy that. This man really is my father. And he doesn't deny it. Why, he's embracing it! Accepting me as* his.

John paused. "It appears the health field runs in our veins. With you, too. It's more than skin deep looks and blue eyes. I can see the apple didn't fall far from the tree. Too bad the tree was half a continent away. I was never the same after my buddy . . . ." He sighed. "Charlie Wong lost his legs, and all I could do was stop the bleeding and get him back to the cop-ter."

Dawn looked at him through new eyes. "Looks like we have more in common than I realized. I have a loss of my own.

The death of my marriage."

"Yes, sorrow is the great equalizer."

He looked into her eyes and patted the arm she offered as she escorted him into their makeshift clinic and turned him over to her staff.

"Marsha is into holistic health, so what can I say? There are definitely inherited traits we all seem to share. Kinda special, isn't it?" He paused, looked at her for a moment, and in a very quiet tone said, "I've never told anyone that part of the story. I think you need to know I feel guilt, remorse, and regret . . . for many things. Parts of me are broken and cracked."

Dawn spoke from her heart. "I am honored you told me. Losses have to see the light of day. The cracks let in the light so healing can take place."

Dawn was rattled, upset that John had issues beyond his cough. He was suspected of having a heart condition. He was getting up there, too — in his seventies now. He'd survived the 1970s, now he had to face his seventies to win against time, age, and COVID-19. He was her father to boot. *This is way more than I can deal with right now. I'm exhausted and can't think straight. I gotta take a break. Thank God for perks as an officer. I can take a break and put myself at ease.*

She walked away from the Lodge and headed down to Elkmont. It was deserted there. When she cleared the encampment at the Lodge, she walked the length of the road until she was deep within the campground. She had ordered tents with cots to be set up just in case, and it appeared that everything was in place. She found the furthest one, and for once, was truly alone. She was happy to see the army blanket and pillow, a quiet spot to unwind. She needed to get away from the disease, the tension, the fatigue, and the emotional complications and just rest in the solitude of the deep wood pines and occasional hemlocks.

The forest was thick here, the air surprisingly warm, and Dawn's uniform felt hot and burdensome. But it was not as quiet as she thought. Birdsong filled the air, and the stream had a voice all its own. Nature calling her to shed her clothes along with her worries. She needed a catnap.

She removed her coat, t-shirt, bra, boots, pants, and skivvies and laid them with military precision at the foot of her cot. She lay in peace, stripped of every care and clothing that weighed her down. She loved the feel of her naked skin against the cool mountain air but covered herself with the army blanket. It certainly wasn't made of Egyptian cotton, but she rested beneath it as if it were. Her worries faded away into a much-needed sleep, where she dreamed of Drew.

She could feel his warmth, the heat of his passion for her, teasing her. His poking and gentle prodding wakened feelings long kept at bay. The curls of his chest hairs caressed her naked breast, increasing the throbbing need building within her, deep in her center. Her wetness lubricated her, and she yearned for the entry of his throbbing dick. She pressed her breasts into his rock-hard furred chest and clutched him with her innermost muscles, and her name bleated from his lips. At least she supposed it was her name, though it sounded more like aaawan than Dawn. She breathed in his scent and felt the rasp of his tongue outlining her lips when his scent reached her nose, and suddenly she felt the hard cold metal of a . . . of a bell? Hell! She heard another guttural sound from deep in his throat. She reached out and . . .

She suddenly woke to find a hairy creature licking her face, and it smelled like a . . . like a goat! Which it was. Well, actually, it was two goats in her tent, making their way out with her clothes!

What in hell? What the fuck were goats doing in the Great Smoky Mountains? And they have my frickin' clothes! They backed out of her tent and bolted — her bra in one goat's mouth and her coat and briefs in the other's. She scampered after them, screeching mad and naked as the blue jay in the pine tree beside her tent. *Who knew goats could run that fast?*

Just then, Drew burst on the scene, gaping at her in all her naked glory.

She screamed. "Don't just stand there, get them. They ran off with my clothes."

He stood rooted to the spot while she ran after them. "Why are you just standing there? Do something."

Drew entered the tent. He ran out with the blanket in hand and attempted to cover her, placing it around her shoulders.

"Don't worry about me. Get my clothes."

"They won't be wearable anymore. Goats eat everything in sight. Those are Sunny's goats, Ashe and Ashley. She adopted them when she found them abandoned after the Chimney Tops Two Wildfire of 2016."

"They have my clothes." She couldn't believe it. The stupid goats would be carrying her undies back to the Lodge, where her unit was. Where her reputation would become the laughingstock of the century. Where her half-eaten briefs and bra would be on display. Questions would follow, even if unvoiced. Speculation would run rampant, and rumors would spread. She'd just have to deal.

"I'll text Eve," Drew offered.

"No can do. I had to isolate her late this afternoon. I got word she tested positive, and I've since learned John has been admitted to our field hospital." Then her carefully constructed walls burst, and she broke down and cried and cried and cried.

Drew gathered her in his arms, blanket and all, and held her. Just held her and let her cry. Her cry turned into humongous ugly sobs that ripped from her throat. And at that moment, she fell in love with him.

In her gut, she knew Eve and John weren't going to fare well. They were sick—seriously sick. Day after day, she struggled with the never-ending stream of suffering humanity that engulfed her team. It was relentless. People out of work, people sick, people hungry. On a twenty-four-seven cycle. But she needed a break from the myriad of needs she faced. She was near her breaking point.

So she let Drew support her, let him hold her, let him comfort her, let him give her his handkerchief, let him love her, and she took all that he offered.

Snuggled in the warmth of his arms, she whispered, "Make love to me."

Drew swept her off her feet and carried her inside the tent, still wrapped in the army blanket. He sat on the cot and held her on his lap. He lit the fire within her by ever so gently, catching her tears with fingertips or lips to kiss them away. He soothed the hair away from her forehead and kissed each eyelid softly, gently, lovingly. His lips met hers, and warm healing and comfort met her at every turn.

He trailed kisses down the column of her neck and gently sucked at the sensitive spots her responses led him to. His tongue outlined the shell of her ear, and his hot breath and body heat spread warmth throughout her. He opened the blanket as he moved her from his lap unto the cot.

She was already naked, so he eased her off the blanket. He rid himself of his clothes and cuddled next to her, kissing her all the while. His hands ran down the length of her, pausing here and there to suck, kiss, or caress.

She felt a fluttering in her gut and didn't fight the feeling. Instead, she surrendered to the feel of his furry chest, the hardness of his corded muscles, the strength of sinew that knit him into the wonderful being captured within skin and bone. Her fingers traced the crags of his chiseled face, stretched to reach his beard, and continue exploring his face.

His brown eyes gazed at her with a look of love, care, and concern.

She couldn't speak.

He kissed her breathless, and she wanted to drown herself in all the promises in his eyes. His face lit up like a Christmas tree when his gaze wandered to her breasts. She gasped when he touched her there. His tongue traced the sensitive area below each nipple until each tightened in response. Then he drew the now straining nipple into his mouth and gently—oh, so sweetly—began to suck.

His hands strayed to her belly and dipped in between the folds of her femininity.

Moisture gathered and pooled between her thighs.

Suddenly, he stopped cold.

"What are you doing?" she gasped.

"We're breaking the social distancing thing."

"Hell, Drew, we both tested negative. Carry on."

He played with her nub, touching her lightly until she stained against his hand and surrendered. Her climax was blinding.

He stilled his hand and let her savor the sensation, wallow in the satisfaction, and when she returned to earth, he whispered, "I have no protection with me."

She squirmed. "Neither do I. The goats ate it. No worries. I'm not ovulating."

"You practice Rhythm? Your body is that regular?"

She laughed. "Rhythm. Haven't heard that one in a long time. Remember the joke?"

"You mean, what do they call people who use Rhythm as birth control?"

She nodded and completed the thought. "Yeah, they call them *parents*." She giggled. "I don't need the pill, a condom, or Rhythm. I'm post-menopausal. I also have no STDs."

"Me neither."

"You're post-menopausal, too, huh?"

He slapped her on the ass. "I have no STDs. Don't we have better things to do with our mouths than talk?" He silenced her with a long, hot, wet, full mouth, heart-stopping series of deep kisses, then entered her.

His eyes widened when he completely submerged, obviously feeling the full onslaught of her internal heating system. He pulled out and leaned away.

He wiped his brow. "That is one helluva hot kitty."

"Brought to you courtesy of my post-menopausal heat at work. My aim is to please."

"Don't you mean tease? Roll over here, closer." She scooted over, and he once again entered her furnace.

He began to move in a rhythmic pace, sliding in, then withdrawing only to plunge into her again and again. She caught his mouth with hers and ate at his lips, driving him faster and faster. Her name tore through his lips as he thrust into her red-hot depths one last time, looking like he just came apart. Just shattered into a million milliseconds of exquisite delight, pleasure, and release.

He held her tight and murmured, "I love you, Dawn. I honestly love you."

She felt safe, secure, and happy in his arms and willingly surrendered to the bliss of the afterglow.

When she awoke, he was gone.

Ain't that just like a man? Disappears after the deed is done. What did you expect? A proposal? The morning mist gathered around the river and spread among the tents and campgrounds, matching her pensive mood. Her eyelids lowered to hide the hope he had inspired with his caresses.

She had to eat her thoughts when Drew, wearing a face shield, returned not only with a boxed hot breakfast but also with fresh fatigues for her to wear.

She couldn't believe her eyes. "How on earth—"

His finger rose to his lips. "Shh. Don't ask, don't tell."

Wordlessly, she took the food and smiled. Suddenly, she rose to her full height, her stance rigid, the box falling from her hands. She froze to the spot, feeling her face drain of color.

Drew just stared at her.

Very, very slowly, an eight-point white buck appeared out of the mist and moved toward her. It dipped its head, dropping something at her feet, then bounded away toward the river.

"Sweet Jesus." At her feet lay her bra and bikini briefs.

Drew gasped. "Did you see that?"

She swallowed hard and nodded. "The Ghost Stag. My skivvies. Holy shit!"

Now she had to worry about was a stupid legend on top of COVID-19, her new family, and her growing feelings for Drew.

Drew looked at her from beneath half-lidded eyes. "Bet you thought I just up and left like a typical man, right?"

She wanted to deny it, but the color she felt rising in her face would belie her words. She lowered her eyelids like window blinds, holding her feelings closely inside. "What makes you think that?"

He came closer, removing his face shield. "Your unfortunate fight with fate. We talked about fate the day we drove here, remember? See, here's an example that something better than River is your fate." He tipped her face to his, removed her mask — crazy goats left that barrier behind — to kiss her lips. "Fate could end up being your best friend."

She borrowed a line from his playbook. "Time will tell." She replaced her mask.

Breakfast completely forgotten, Drew donned his face shield and bent to pick up the food containers to pack them out. A smile crossed his face and his dimples deepened.

She had to smile at his actions. *Leave nothing but footprints behind.*

He pressed further. "Admit it. We both want more than a toss beneath the blanket. You didn't ask me to fuck you or screw you. You said *make love to me.* And that's what last night was all about. Not screwing around, but making love."

God help me, but this crazy heart of mine just skipped a beat. Something like happiness soared through her. Once again — ignoring social distancing — she ran to him, wanting to land a big, hot kiss on his luscious, juicy, and waiting lips. When she did, his face shield clinked, and they broke apart, laughing. *That's what I get for breaking the rules.*

He swiped his fingers, making a *shame, shame* gesture at her.

Chapter Ten: Rain Keeps Falling

Molly woke up that morning and decided she was bored silly and beginning to chafe at the quarantine way of life. She had been a trooper. Dawn had said as much. She did the usual stuff, and her iPad was entertaining, but not enough. *Thank God for YouTube, but even that is not cutting it.*

She tried exercising to a Pilates YouTube but was still restless. She had been fishing, hiking, and hanging out with Jake, messing with his guitar here and there, but she needed something *more* to do. Puzzles and crosswords were one thing, but not enough now. *Old fogies, like Uncle Drew, rely on them, not me.* She figured he was already working, so she left him a note.

Didn't Jake say there was a hike to a nearby waterfall, Meigs Falls or sumthin'? Maybe I can get him, and we can hike through the mist. It'll be an adventure. I'll check my sugar and see how I'm doin', then see if I can find him.

Molly checked her sugar and found she needed to eat. Fortunately, her breakfast came with orange juice to drink should she need it. She placed the bottle along with power bars into her backpack and then took her insulin shot. *Diabetes is no joy. Gawd, I hate this stupid disease. I'm grateful for insulin and all but . . . Giving myself a shot is no picnic in the woods.* She looked around her at the soaring second forest growth. She grinned at her wordplay and went to find Jake.

Good thing I don't have to take another shot until bedtime. I'm going to talk to Uncle Drew and Mom and see what they think of an insulin pump. Who knows when I'll be able to see my doctor with all this COVID closing so many places?

When she found Jake, he looked as out of sorts as she felt. He was sitting on the picnic table bench outside of Jump Over the Moon Cabin, kicking up loose pebbles and sending them off to who knows where. *He's draggin' his wagon, too.*

"Hey, Jake. Wassup?"

"Not much."

Molly kicked at the dirt, too. "Same here. I'm so bored. I was thinkin' . . . Why don't we go on that hike you were telling me about?"

Jake perked up. "That's not a bad idea. I think the rain will hold off. It can rain in the mountains in one spot and be dry around the bend. I'll tell Mom and meet you at the fountain. Better change shoes."

"Crocs are good if we have to cross a stream."

Jake shrugged. "It's your funeral. No complaints if you regret it. At least wear your hoodie."

She pointed to her waist. She was wearing it tied around her so it was within reach and would be easy to get into. She also drew Jake's attention to her backpack. "Got some OJ and power bars."

"Sick."

She sniggered and headed for the fountain.

Jake found his mother absorbed in some book called *Promises on the Beach* and told her their plan.

His mother nodded. "Don't go far. Stay on the trail. We're in the wilderness, you know."

"Yeah, yeah. I got it. Be careful. Yadda, yadda, yadda."

Moments later, he walked down to the fountain on the front lawn of the Lodge. Noting the wishing well not far away, he tossed in a coin and wished for something he couldn't really put a name to. He decided to wish for good fortune.

Once Molly joined him, Jake led the way. He had a map he had snatched from the Lodge and pointed the way. "We get there by following the road."

Molly, bending to look at the map, said, "We'll cut off some miles if we cross the stream and pick the trail up here." Her finger pointed to the route she meant. "If we cross downstream, we can use the rocks like a bridge and rock hop across the stream. It's just a trickle, and if we hit a soaker, no biggie. My Crocs can handle it. Don't know if your fancy footwear will, but no complaining if you soak your Nikes."

Jake grinned and nodded. "Epic."

He led them along the stream to where a small island with a few trees that somehow managed to grow through the thin, rocky soil split the river. It looked a bit easier to cross from there.

Once on the other side, there was a fork in the trail created by numerous hikers.

"Go left," Molly said. "I think the steeper trail must drop off somewhere along the river to create the falls."

There wasn't a lot of tree cover. The leaves were still in the infant stage and not yet fully grown to offer any protection. The mountain air was filled with the scent of cedar and pine unique to the hills. The fragrance was wonderful, fresh, clean, and pure. Weak sunlight peeked between dull gray clouds and seemed to shimmer in the dissolving mist.

Jake laughed when Molly twirled in joy, holding her arms heavenward.

"This is what I'm talking about," she crowed.

The trail headed up, and they continued to climb.

Deborah figured Jake was most likely eating with Molly when he missed lunch. Knowing her son, they probably poached some lunch from Millie's cabin and planned to make a picnic out of their walk. But when it was time for supper, and he still had yet to return, she looked for Beau to see if Jake was with him. Maybe they were whittling together.

It didn't take long to discover that Jake was not with Beau.

Deborah wrung her hands. "I never should have let him go on a hike with Molly. I thought they were just walking that Quiet Walkway down the road. I should have known better."

Beau chuckled. "How many times have we told him to take a hike?"

Deborah wasn't swayed. His lame attempt at humor didn't land well.

Beau tried to calm her fears. "The kid's not stupid. He'll be all right."

"He's fifteen! He's with a girl. He's not thinking of anything but impressing her. He's not all right. If he were, he'd be home for dinner, for God's sake. It's my fault. I never should have agreed. I'll never forgive myself if . . ." Tears slipped down her face. Her breath came out in gasps.

Beau moved toward her and patted her shoulder. She was rigid with stark fear bordering on panic that his attempt at comfort couldn't quell.

"We need to let Second Lieutenant Winters know and contact Drew," Beau suggested. "Where'd Jake say he was going?"

"Some falls. A Girl's name. Meg's Falls? Something like that."

"That's got to be near here. They wouldn't go far, especially since it looks like rain."

Deborah followed Beau to the Lodge to notify Second Lieutenant Winters. She listened with growing alarm spreading through her, dread settling in her heart and stomach.

Sunny spoke up from behind the reception desk. "That's Meigs Falls. You can get there using the road. Well, from here, you have to ford the river, but that's not terribly far from here, and the stream is low." She pointed to the lamp, recently lit by the automatic sensors. "They're bound to come back, since it's night now."

"The stream *was* low. The recent rain forced me outta my tent, remember?" Beau reminded.

"Thank God, the falls are close," Deborah muttered.

Sunny handed Beau a copy of the National Park's Guide with a map of the area. She pointed to the section the kids had said they were headed for.

Beau moved fast. "Let's go. I'll get my truck."

"That'll be a *no*." The Second Lieutenant's tone brooked no argument. "My job. You're in quarantine, remember? And you aren't trained for this. I'll handle it. Excuse me. Just return to your quarters, and trust we'll find them."

Beau led Deborah outside as vehement protests fell from her choked throat. "There's wild animals out there, Beau!"

"I know. We can't do anything here. The Second Lieutenant's right, we don't know the terrain. I gotta text Drew to let him know what's going on."

Before Beau could finish the text, Drew joined the group standing at the Visitors Desk. Sunny handed him a copy of the park's newspaper and opened it, drawing his attention to the map and trail.

Drew's face was lined with worry. He showed the group the note Molly had left behind. The anguish in his eyes bespoke his fears. He didn't have to say a thing. Deborah knew exactly what he was feeling.

Then in a deadly calm voice, Drew said, "Molly has Diabetes. She could go into insulin shock."

Deborah was shocked when the Second Lieutenant flew to Drew's side, apparently not caring about social distancing.

"Trust me, Drew. We'll find them." She stepped away from the group and radioed Luke Scraper, the ranger.

Luke had notified the National Park Search and Rescue

Unit to form a search team. After several hours, the search team returned and shook their head.

"It's begun to rain hard again," the team leader said. "Another spring storm. Happens here all the time. Visibility is low, the trail is washed out, and it's too dangerous to use the helicopter. We'll have to wait until morning's first light. Let's pray this deluge ends."

The rain continued to fall, as if trying to reclaim the Earth. Deborah's panic was growing in leaps and bounds. *I can't lose another child.*

She almost laughed hysterically when she heard the Second Lieutenant wishing she had an ark to carry those who needed it to a better place. That was followed with a muttered, "Now if we can just find those kids . . . no, when we find those kids, I'm going to court-martial them."

Molly was tiring. She desperately needed to eat. The lunch Jake had managed to secure was long gone. She knew she had power bars and orange juice, but they could hardly stop now to rummage through her backpack to get them. They had to get back to the cabins.

The trail grew steeper, and rain began to fall. Jake looked up at the rapidly darkening skies. "I didn't think the falls were this far away. The rain's gonna get worse."

Lightning struck a nearby tree, causing Molly to clutch Jake.

"We must have missed a turn. We're turning back. We'll just retrace our steps."

Molly agreed. "Yeah. Totally." She raised a hand to her head, feeling dizzy and a little dazed. Lightheaded or something. *I don't want to think about it. Did this hiking use up my insulin somehow? The extra exertion?*

But then the clouds flashed along with the thunder and let loose. They ran back down the slippery slope looking fearfully over their shoulders at the trail washing away in the torrent, becoming a stream in its own right. Rainwater began filling the once quiet stream, changing it into a raging, roaring river. A river that was impossible to cross now. They had no choice but to go forward to find the falls where they could be seen from the road.

"My idea wasn't a good one," she muttered. "We should have taken the road after all."

"Never mind. It is what it is. How could we know? We gotta find shelter." Jake grabbed her hand.

Lightning flashed, revealing an overhang of rock and dirt. They scrambled to get beneath it. Molly removed her wet shirt and zipped up her hoodie. Wearing just the hoodie and her beyond wet leggings, she tucked her cold feet under herself, wishing she had socks.

When lightning flashed again, Jake looked terrified. Molly huddled as close as she could to him as they crouched under the overhang and tried to stay warm. She felt so out of it. *I'm crashing. Need OJ.*

She moaned and somehow croaked the words, "Diabetes . . . OJ . . ."

Jake dug through her things, found it, opened the container by inserting the attached straw, and raised it to her lips.

"Call for help. Try nine-one-one," she suggested.

"I don't have many bars left." He tried calling nine-one-one but couldn't get through. "Maybe I should try to hike out and lead them back here."

"No. Don't leave me. I feel sick. Kind of woozy."

"Okay. We'll try to stay here. Crouch in there and put your back to the outside. Curl up. I'm gonna get pine branches to block the wind. Maybe that way we can keep our core warm."

"You some kind of boy scout?"

Jake merely grinned. "Yup."

Fortunately, he managed to use some downed brush to

form a shelter, and they rationed the last protein bar.

CHAPTER ELEVEN: AIN'T NO SUNSHINE

Things had been running like clockwork, if Dawn thought in terms of her unit distributing food, transporting people, COVID testing, and performing their mission. But personally, things were disturbing, much like the weather.

Spring in the Smokies, like elsewhere, brought unpredictable changes in weather and moods. Big swings in the atmospheric pressure caused feeling to rush, cascade, ebb, flow, and churn. Dark clouds promising rain swelled within the mountain sky. When she checked on Eve, Dawn had kicked Eve's COVID partner, Beau Jobs, out of their cabin and into the recently established campground tents so she could isolate Eve. But he'd gotten washed out with the rain and was now staying with his ex and son.

Eve wasn't doing well. If she got worse, Dawn would have to admit her to their field hospital. In fact, she'd already had John transported there, and he wasn't improving. Despite its poor reputation and results, she was tempted to try hydroxychloroquine despite knowing it wasn't effective. But its known heart risks made it impossible to use on John. *I'd try voodoo if that was feasible – anything that could help.*

Good thing I called for an additional medical team just days ago. COVID's reach had not caught her by surprise. Already, they were treating three people. Two were military, one was John, and now Eve might well become the fourth.

They had been using every medical weapon in their arsenal. The medical staff kept in frequent contact with officials of the CDC, the Department of Health, as well as the Governor.

The last time Dawn had seen Eve, she'd given her a radio and taught her how to use it. She ordered that Eve's vitals be taken hourly. Deep down, she knew Eve was worse than ever. In all her years with her sister, she had never seen her this bad. Coughing, wheezing, and she actually whistled when she took a breath.

Every free moment Dawn had and late into each night, she read the latest research on her tablet. The promise of a vaccine was months out. That wasn't the answer for her sister or any of them. They were sick right here, right now. A vaccine was simply not available. She'd have to make do with what she knew, researched, and could lay her hands on.

Remdesivir and Ribavirin, as well as other medicines like dexamethasone, were in use in some places. Other doctors recommended and used a cocktail of drugs, including steroids. Some research reports showed twenty percent of those intubated often died. Some victims did heal on their own, but there was no clear information as to why those patients had while others had not.

Dawn studied everything she could to fight this disease, not only to help her military family but also her own flesh and blood, and now two of those were here under her care. In a pinch, she would plead with the doctors to try a drug cocktail before they had to consider intubation. Fortunately, no one else in her unit, the Lodge, or the cabins, had tested positive.

She wished Molly and Jake were safe and in their cabins. They were more at risk of the weather now than anything else. She crossed her fingers and prayed for the best. She had done everything she could for Molly and Jake. She could only hope they were found soon or showed up themselves.

Dawn reviewed Eve's chart on her tablet. Eve's temp was now 104 and rising. Dawn's stomach churned with worry and apprehension. She was frightened to her very core. *My other half, my twin.*

Early the next morning, Dawn received the call she had been dreading.

"Mayday, Dawn. I'm bad," Eve croaked.

"Hang on. I've got you." Dawn replied over the static of the radio.

She grabbed her other radio and called for a medivac team. She moved as fast as she and her team could in the cloudburst of activity. She had her hands full with handling Eve's care, working on pure adrenaline.

"Move, move, move," she repeatedly told her staff.

Finally, she got everything hooked up, and her team took over. She was shaking with anxiety, yet could not, would not show any signs of it. She held her hands when they weren't in use to prevent their shaking. *I can manage this. I can do this* became her focus and her mission.

After she'd gotten Eve stabilized, still shaking but out of view of those under her command, she paused, remembering the scene she'd met when Eve was removed from her cabin. Her mind played and replayed the scenario, reliving the entire ordeal.

Eve on a stretcher. A tarp over her to shield her from the rain. Tears leaking from her twins' eyes. Fear in those blue eyes. Eve, undone, perhaps sick unto death. Eve stripped of her sweats, lost beneath the shapeless, horrid hospital gown. Eve lying next to the long windows in the Banquet Room, now a field hospital housing four sick souls. The doctor, rushing in, trying to save her sister.

Eve clutching at her throat, struggling to catch a breath, a cannula placed in her nostrils, tubes, and IVs lining her arms. Drugs flowing in.

A medic, who was assisting, saying, "She's suffering from delirium, Second Lieutenant Winters. Our options are narrowing. I've treated her fever. Let's pray it works."

There was no more she could do. It was in God's hands.

Exhausted, Dawn went upstairs to her room and prayed.

She found her rosary and began reciting the Apostles Creed, Our Fathers, and Hail Marys. How she'd ever learned them was unclear and didn't matter at the moment. She needed the mindless repetition. She said them by rote. It seemed to ease her worries and gave her something constructive to do when she could do no more. She tried to get some rest, but she tossed and turned, her thoughts tumbling like pebbles down the rainy path outside the Lodge.

The next morning, she put herself on the Sick Bay duty, assisting the doctors and patients they had under care. She turned the distribution of food and transport over to a team leader to focus her energy on dealing with her COVID cases. She was confident that her unit knew what to do and how to do it.

Fortunately, the quasi-quarantine, isolating, and social distancing appeared to be working for the most part. *So far*, Mountain Heritage Hospital was not overwhelmed, and for that, she was grateful. But still, Eve labored to breathe.

Despite all she did, Dawn had no other choice. Either she tried the experimental drug cocktail before it was too late, or they'd have to intubate. John had already been placed on a ventilator that thankfully they had secured. They only had two machines. She prayed Eve wouldn't need one. She worried about Eve and John and pleaded with the doctor to try the cocktail.

He reluctantly reminded her, "It's experimental. We don't know if it'll do the trick." Exhaustion flooded his eyes, and his gaze suggested it might not work.

The cocktail they had decided to use with Eve consisted of administering three pills taken orally over several hours. They had opened the windows to allow air to circulate. Good ole fashioned fresh mountain air and modern drugs and a miracle, and maybe just maybe, Eve and John could make it.

She propped Eve up and gave her the medicine while Eve could still swallow. Remdesivir had to be administered soon. It might be too late to use if they waited any longer. Everything that could be done was being done. She even arranged for the proning procedure to occur on a strict schedule.

Her thoughts turned to the missing hikers. *Now, if we can just find Molly and Jake . . . no,* when *we find those kids, I'm going to Velcro them to their fathers. At least then I'll know where they are.*

Worry tore through her.

CHAPTER TWELVE: HELP I NEED SOME-ONE

Drew knew Beau was doing his best to calm and console Deborah, but that wasn't his concern. *I have to think, do something. There has to be a way to find them.* Then his job kicked in, and he went into full communication mode. *Maybe Molly wore a tracker to help her manage her diabetes. For sure, they both had phones. Molly never goes anywhere without hers, not sure about Jake. If they tried to call nine-one-one, that would help. Nine-one-one calls are designed to connect to the nearest tower, and I can trace that. Don't know if the weather and the mountains will interfere with transmission.*

He began the search using his iPhone. *We have a family plan. Maybe I can find out where they are. Get their coordinates. It's worth a try. I can mess with the bandwidth and cell towers. There's one in Wears Valley . . . maybe just maybe.*

He texted Beau.

Jake have a tracker? Phone?

Yes.

Get over to the Lodge.

Drew and Beau worked their magic. They set up tracers for both of the kid's phones and for Jake's fitness tracker. It felt like forever, but after a few moments, they found a faint signal. Something. At last.

Drew immediately radioed the data to Ranger Luke Scraper. Dawn had told him that Luke had search and rescue experience and had made arrangements to join the search party.

Luke called him a few minutes later. "The team is uploading your data to their GPSs and checking their maps. Little River is no longer a mere picturesque stream, it's become a raging river. We're gathering cinches, rope throw bags, and other gear we'll need, but we'll be ready to head out first thing in the morning."

Judging by the fear Drew saw in everyone's eyes, no one associated with the Lodge would get much sleep that night.

In the morning, Drew paced as the Search and Rescue Team gathered their wetsuits, harnesses, helmets, water shoes, and other gear. Beau and Deborah stood nearby while Luke explained how the teams were going to conduct the rescue.

"A helicopter will drop small teams on each side of the river as close to the signal as they can," Luke said. "Another team will be taking an army vehicle on Little River Road, since it has the closest and the easiest access to Meigs Falls. That's the team I'll be with. We'll all fan out from our drop-off points, then begin our search for the kids."

Jake was just as scared when he woke as he had been the night before. Molly split their last half of the power bar, but he insisted she drink the rest of the orange juice. It was clear she needed it more than he did. It had stopped raining momentarily, but a frosty mist and their wet clothing had them both shivering.

"Let's stay on what most looks like a trail and try to find the road," he suggested.

Molly voiced a weak protest. "Last night, you wanted to hike back the way we came."

Jake shrugged. "I think since we're probably close to the falls, chances are we'll be seen from the road. That way, we can flag down help."

Molly's teeth were chattering, and a series of shivers made her discomfort clear. "That makes sense. Things always look better after you sleep on it. Well, in our case, maybe . . . Since we got a chance to rest and think, we can now follow a better plan. This was a dumb idea. I'm sorry." She offered a small apologetic smile.

Jake shook his head in surprise. "*We* made a decision. No one dragged me into anything."

The trail was full of slick wet roots, mud, and water. The path looked more like a stream to Jake. He followed the flow of water, which ran downhill like a waterfall. It felt like they'd been hiking for hours, and most probably they had.

It was evident Molly just didn't have the strength to continue. She had missed two insulin shots, and her appearance had Jake worried. Her eyes closed, and she sagged against a spruce tree, its needles scant protection against the worsening conditions.

Jake found a log she could huddle against underneath a sparsely branched spruce tree. He left her there with his Tennessee orange letter jacket, hoping it would help keep her warm. He figured he'd work up body heat with the hike ahead of him.

He crossed his fingers as he hiked, hoping he was going in the right direction. When he finally spotted the road across the river, he started yelling and screaming, waving his light-gray hoodie from side to side overhead.

The winds whistled through the leafless branches as if they too were screeching. Cold rain poured, making footing treacherous as if things weren't already bad enough. The higher elevation chilled the air, and the temperature dropped even lower. Jake finally saw some people and recognized Ranger Luke Scraper. He yelled louder to catch their attention.

Luke was the first to spot him. "There he is! Across the river."

The rescuers got busy with their equipment. They yelled directions to him, but the roar of the river drowned out their words. They used a sort of sign language and tossed a throw bag at him.

Jake caught the throw bag, opened it, and donned the harness. He cinched it to what he assumed was a guideline, then entered the water.

A member of the team—using a cinch and the other end of the guideline—met Jake about halfway across the river.

As the guy got nearer, he yelled out, "Put the throw bag over your left shoulder and point your feet downstream."

Jake wished he had a wet suit and helmet, too, but he didn't. The force of the freezing water was stronger than his own fear, which made him automatically take a breath and keep going.

Jake's teeth were chattering when he finally reached the safety of the shore. He was shaking with cold and anxiety. They wrapped him up like a burrito in a foil blanket, and he wished he were as warm as a baked potato.

"Molly's up the r-right fork on the t-trail," he stuttered. "She looked bad last time I saw her. I had to leave her behind."

Luke's voice reassured him. "You did the right thing. We might not have found you, otherwise." He ordered the team to take Jake home.

When Jake got home, shaking with cold, his parents hugged him within an inch of his life. Millie clucked around him, holding a mug of hot chicken soup out to him while ordering his dad to get a blanket and fetch dry clothes.

Luke radioed Molly's location to the other team and headed

to meet up with them. When he found Molly, the other guys were already on the scene. Molly had passed out and was unresponsive. He called the helicopter for a pickup. They would need the airlift to get her to the hospital as quick as possible.

"Check her blood sugar level," Luke told the rescuers. "Her uncle mentioned she has Type One diabetes and may not have brought her insulin with her."

The guy with the first aid kit pulled out a tester to check. "Her blood sugar level is really low. She's gone into a diabetic coma." He immediately gave her a shot of glucagon to raise her sugar levels.

"Her heart rate is low, too," another guy called out.

When the helicopter arrived, the team carefully secured Molly and escorted her to Blount County Hospital. They continued to perform CPR during the flight, each member of the team taking over when others grew tired. No one gave up, and they used every weapon in their arsenal.

Luke was watching the heart monitor when it suddenly went erratic. "She's gone AFib! Bag her. Get the defibrillator."

"We're in flight!"

"Do it. That's an order," Luke growled.

Molly was stabilized by the time they landed. They were met by a team of hospital personnel, who hovered over her too-still body. Luke followed them inside and pulled out his cellphone to call and update Drew.

The last thing Molly remembered was feeling dizzy and lightheaded, kinda floaty. And then she was actually floating! She watched the scene below as the rescue workers bent over her body, but she wasn't in her body. She was rising up, up, and almost away. She was floating above it all, feeling wonderful.

They seemed to be frantically doing things to her body, cuffing it with the blood pressure doodad and stabbing her with needles. She didn't feel the compressions. She didn't feel the needles. She felt nothing.

Then suddenly, she was overwhelmed with a sense of freedom and joy. No longer cold. No more teeth chattering. No shivers. She gazed back at her body and noticed her blue lips, and her coloring was terrible. *Yikes. I need some serious makeup.*

Feel good now. Feel free. Feel light. Feel happy.

Folks in the copter, all around me. They don't look happy. They're frantic. Yelling things. Beating my chest. Quit it, guy. I'm happy. Peaceful. It's so pretty here. Man, the colors are brilliant. Light and color and music surround me. It's so cool.

People smiling. So friendly. Profound love enveloping me, flowing through me, and embracing me. Leave me be, guys. I want to stay here.

I look down at all the frenzy. The people jammed into the helicopter, so upset. There's IV bags and medical stuff. Shots. I don't feel any of it. They are trying hard to get me to . . . No, I don't want to. They want me to stay with them, hang in there, stay there. Then I hear someone yell, Stat!

Someone is shoving something down my throat. Chill, peeps. I'm fine. Really. I wanna be here. Everyone is so nice here. It's so easy. I can float and do such cool stuff. The light is so bright. I'm drawn to it. It's pure love. I wrap myself within it.

Hey, Mom's here! She's way rad, radiant with light shimmering around her. She's dressed in white, and she's glowing.

Mom! Whatcha doin' here, Mom? *She's so bright. She's filled with light like me. Happy, warm, loving light! I think it, and here she is beside me. We're together. I'm so happy.*

Mom's happy, too.

We run in this great big field. Man, the colors are outta this world.

Mom's trying to tell me something. She stops me.

No, I tell her gently. I smile with my soul, not my mouth. How am I doing that? I like it here.

Her lips don't move, but she's telling me it's her *time to be here,* not *mine. She* needs *to be here. I have to go* back. *We aren't even using words. We talk but don't need our mouth to do it. Ya think it, and presto, the other one hears. How cool is that?*

Mom argues with me, *saying Uncle Drew needs me.*

No, he doesn't.

It's not your time yet.

Yes, it is. This is *my time. I* need *to be here with you. Like always. You and me and Uncle Drew.*

She tells me she crossed over. Something about a roadside bomb.

That's okay, I reply. I can deal. You're with me. I've missed you so much.

She says there's a plan for me, and I have to follow it. My purpose or something.

What's she saying? I'll do my plan from here. I'll stay with you right here. We'll do more cool things together.

She tells me Uncle Drew needs me. And he needs Dawn. Dawn's been chosen just for him.

I'm supposed to go back now. I'm supposed to tell Uncle Drew that Dawn was made just for him. Soulmates?

Soulmates? For reals?

Mom says she doesn't really want to show me this, but . . . . She shows me this darling little girl. Oh, how I love her! So much love for this girl. She's so pretty and so bright. But wait — what's happening to her? Her light is fading, dimming, and growing dimmer and dimmer. Stop! Don't go. Don't fade . . .

Moms says, if I don't go back with Uncle Drew, this girl will never be born. She'll be here . . . maybe.

What? Say What? She can just stay here like us, I point out.

Mom says the beautiful little soul with her long golden locks is going to be my *little girl someday, and she's going to cure Diabetes.*

Whoa. That gets my attention.

Mom says I have work to do and that I've met my soulmate already. And I have to go back and help Uncle Drew. Wowser.

Then she shows me Jake. He's a man now — no earrings, no piercings, no Mohawk, no purple hair. Man is he built! He's ripped. His abs are outta sight. He's so good looking! He's my soulmate? My soulmate? Dope!

Mom tells me I saw the Ghost Stag, and Jake was there, too, but I didn't see him. He saw the Stag as well. Only soulmates can see him.

Mom asks if I get it now. I have stuff to do. I hafta go back.

No! I don't want to. I love Mom so much. I don't want to leave her. Then I remember how smokin' Jake was. I think of the cure for Diabetes. That darling little girl. My daughter.

Mom says I'll see her again. She'll always be keeping her eye on me. I know that's true somehow, someway I understand. I feel it. It's as real as this place is. This incredible place. It's so gorgeous. The bright jewel colors. Turquoise and pearl, like I've never seen before. And blue waters that sparkle in the most beautiful light I've ever seen . . .

Shit, I'm back! I feel like heck. This is not fun. At all. I'm cold. I hurt. Something's gagging me. I slam into something that feels as hard as concrete, and I'm so heavy. I wake up. I'm not where I was. Something is going beep . . . beep . . . beep. It's flippin' bothering me. So noisy here. It gives me a headache. I feel heavy, like I'm weighed down with a ton of river rock around my neck.

Then I remember Marre, my daughter. Her name is Marre . . . after my mom. I know now, my mom is gone from life on Earth. She's in a different place, one so much better. I can deal. I know where she is. I'll see her again . . . Leaving her makes me weep. But I'm back, and I feel terrible.

Drew was beside himself with worry for Molly. That feeling compounded when two uniformed military personnel knocked on the Lodge door. He took one look and knew—things were already bad and about to get worse. One of the officers said something about a chaplain and kept talking, but his mind was in a haze.

Someone urged him toward a chair, and he fell into it. His mind latched onto occasional words like *purple heart* and *IED* and *gold star*. Then it hit him. His sister, Private First Class Marianne Sunrise, was dead. Molly's mother was dead, and Molly was missing. *Have I lost them both? My little sister is dead. Maryanne's gone.* Grief tore through him. *Molly, how do I tell Molly? When do I tell her? How can I hide it? My heart is broken. How do I carry on?*

He stared blankly as Dawn took over. The next thing he knew, she was handing him something and told him to drink it. Someone's phone was ringing somewhere. He saw Dawn's lips moving, felt Beau draw him into a hug, and heard a gut-wrenching wail. It took a long time for him to realize the agonizing, god-awful sound had ripped from *his* throat. In utter and complete anguish, tears cascaded down his cheeks.

Dawn called for a blanket, and Millie draped it over his shoulders. Through it all, the downpour continued, both from his tears and the rain coming down by the bucket-full outside. *I can't frickin' function. Can hardly breathe.*

Dawn flew into action. She had answered Drew's phone, and Luke had said they'd found Molly but had to rush her to the hospital. She made some quick calls to arrange visitation. Now she just had to get Drew moving.

"Drew, we have to go. Come on. Give him more of that Tennessee Whiskey. He's in shock." She slapped him in the face. Hard. "Drew, get goin'. We have to go to Blount Hospital in Marysville. They found Molly. She's had an insulin reaction. It was touch and go, but they've got her stabilized. Shape up."

He snapped out of his daze, moving his jaw side to side. "You hit me."

"Yes, sir, I did. Get in the Jeep. Get your shit together."

Drew shaped up and straightened his spine. "I'll drive."

She glared at him. "Not this time."

He surrendered. "Fine. You drive."

"Once upon a time, a good man drove me to base. Now, a good woman will return the favor. You wanna do something? Then pray like you never have before."

"Yes, ma'am."

Drew became quiet as Dawn drove the road's twists and turns, the roaring river making talking impossible. *There's not much to say. His sister's gone, and Molly's condition is unknown.*

"I called ahead," Dawn announced. "You and I can see her. COVID hasn't hit hard here yet, or at least Marysville isn't a hotspot. I used every connection I have, pulled rank, and we can get inside to see her."

Drew nodded and bowed his head.

Dawn nodded encouragingly. *Good, it looks like he's praying. How I love this man.*

Chapter Thirteen: A Higher Love

Dawn glanced over at Drew and saw — not for the first time — just what made this man beside her so special. He was honest. Real. Caring. Devoted to family, and at this moment, completely heartbroken. It hurt to see his body wrenching with sobs that shook the long length of him, but he had been sucker-punched to his very soul.

When they reached the hospital, the change in weather was startling. It was as if it hadn't been pouring rain for a day and a half. The sun was shining through the clouds, revealing a spectacular view.

Dawn nudged him with her elbow. "Look at that, Drew." She pointed to the double rainbow hanging over the hospital. "The worst is over. That rainbow has to mean something . . ."

Drew said, "It means light is split like a prism —"

She slugged him — hard. "It's God's apology for taking Marianne and His promise for tomorrow."

Drew rubbed his shoulder and looked thoughtful.

Dawn knew he had been praying. She had ordered him to do so, after all. "You know as well as I do mountain weather ranges far and wide. Drenching downpours on one side of the mountain and sunshine on the other. Those rainbows are a sign . . . A good sign. Admit it. You're the one who believes in fate and destiny, after all."

"Touché. I hope you're right."

Dawn dropped him off at the Emergency Entrance, then parked nearby using military privilege. At the entrance to the hospital, someone was there to take her temperature. She was asked the standard questions. Was she sick? Had she been near anyone diagnosed with COVID? Had she been tested? She replied *yes* to the last two questions and briefly explained her rank and mission.

"I rapid tested negative this morning," she added.

Drew had apparently already passed through the hospital checkpoint. She found him talking with a nurse, and he beckoned her to his side. They were escorted through the doors that opened with a whoosh and ushered through a carefully chosen maze of plastic sheeting. Huge Xs on the floor indicated where folks were to stand for proper social distance. The nurse handed them stacks with gowns, gloves, face shields, and new masks.

Dawn removed the mask she was wearing, placed it in her cargo pants pocket, used the replacements, then slipped the gown over her clothes. Drew followed suit.

Finally, properly attired, she watched the color leach out of Drew's face as he was led to Molly's bedside. He reached his latex-gloved hand out to Molly and held her hand.

Dawn checked Molly's chart, and her hands shook when she read the copter notes. Molly had indeed crashed. She had been considered clinically dead for about thirty minutes, kept alive with CPR. Yet here she was, looking at Molly, who was breathing on her own!

Had Dawn not been a believer, what she now witnessed would have convinced her beyond a doubt that a Higher Power had been in play. Her hands shook harder, making the chart miss the holder at the door, and she tried to steady them to replace the folder. Truly, Molly was a miracle. She had technically died, after all.

In a happy turn of events, Molly was tested using her saliva and did not have COVID. They transported her to an observation area that was well away from the Emergency Room and nowhere near the COVID Intensive Care.

Molly was admitted to the hospital, so Drew checked into the Executive Lodge and ate — fittingly — at the Hot Rod 50s Diner, which was within walking distance.

Since Dawn's mission encompassed the area surrounding Townsend, she was able to see Molly and Drew each day. Blount Memorial Hospital was close, as the crow flew. She frequently stayed late into the night, resting with Drew and supporting him. They didn't make love, but they cuddled whenever possible. As strong as the current between them ran, they were emotionally and physically simply too worn out to do more than murmur words of comfort. Dawn wanted no possibility of impropriety to intrude and wasn't ready to express her feelings out loud.

One late afternoon, Drew said, "I want more from our relationship."

"Now?"

He looked at her with red-rimmed eyes. "We're adults. We've been on the planet long enough to know what love is, but I feel you're holding back. Your past, divorce, and maybe Daddy-issues have made you retreat into a cage. You hold the key to it. Unlock your cage and let me in. Your father wasn't there, but I'm here, right now."

She drew in a breath. "This is hardly the time to discuss this."

"If not now, then when?"

She struggled to rein in her temper. "Not when we're dealing with life and death."

"This is the life and death of *us*. What more do you need from me? I love you. I want to be with you. We've been through hell, but we've got something real here. Deal with it."

Dawn did not stay to cuddle and comfort him that night. She had too much on her mind.

Drew's emotions were raw, but Dawn had Eve and John's COVID to deal with.

Days passed. Dawn went to the hospital daily, but she stopped staying any longer than necessary. She drove back alone each night.

Molly made steady progress, and Eve was beginning to turn the corner. John Weathers was still sick and not at all out of the woods.

At last, the day arrived when Molly could come home.

When Drew saw Dawn the day of Molly's release, he still had not told Molly of Marianne's death. "How can I tell her?"

Dawn was matter of fact. "How can you not?"

Drew spread his hands out in desperation and chewed his lower lip. "I don't want her to have a setback."

Dawn humphed. "She's not stupid. The time for worrying over her is over. She knows you are still upset. You don't want her thinking you are mad at her, disappointed in her, or mad at Jake."

"Why would I be mad at Jake?"

Dawn looked exasperated and blew the air out of her lungs in a huge whoosh. "I know you're not. But Molly doesn't know that. Teenagers think everything is about them and is somehow their fault. If there's drama, that's even better. She'll think all sorts of things until you set her straight."

Drew completed the check-out process at the motel, and Dawn drove him the short distance to the hospital and waited outside. She handed him the duffle bag with a change of clothes for Molly.

When the lengthy discharge process ended, an orderly helped Molly into a wheelchair.

She balked. "I can walk. I'm not an invalid."

The orderly winked. "They all say that. Hospital procedures, dig?"

When they exited the hospital, Dawn was waiting to pick

them up. Drew knew by the way Molly was chattering that she was happy and healthy. He still worried because he had not yet discussed the loss of Marianne with her.

When they approached Meigs Falls, Molly asked Dawn to stop the car and pull over in the small parking area. Molly got out of the Jeep and wrapped her arms around herself even though the spring day was warm.

Her slim body shivered in the sunlight. "This is Meigs Falls, isn't it? It's as pretty as Jake said it'd be. Looks harmless now, doesn't it? This is where Jake and I were headed that day?"

Drew and Dawn got out too and rested against the Jeep as Molly looked around the area.

"Yes, it is." Drew grew concerned, and in a quieter voice, asked, "How much do you remember?"

"I remember the bad parts . . . The damp and cold. The getting lost. The helicopter part was really weird, but in a good way, ya know?"

Drew shook his head. "Tell me."

Molly chewed her bottom lip. "Promise you won't think I'm cray-cray."

Dawn laughed. "That is one thing you are not. I wouldn't encourage a military career for you if you showed any evidence of crazy."

Nodding that she understood, Molly spoke in a soft tone. "I know about Mom, Uncle Drew. I can deal. Truly even though we can't see her, she's alive and well where she is. She said she'd look out for us." She winked. "You know, put in a good word for us to the powers that be."

Drew straightened, shifted his stance, but was too moved to speak.

"Don't worry. Don't be upset. Mom came to me, or I went to her. I'm not sure which. But I know she's not here—with us—anymore. She told me about the IED, you know. She didn't report anything bad. She's good and in a really good place."

Confounded but cautious, Drew asked, "Come again?" That was all he could get out. Unshed tears clogged his tear ducts, and he choked up.

Molly continued in a dream-like tone. "I think I, like, uh, how do I say this? I think I died and went somewhere. You know, to where Mom is now."

Dawn took her hand and just held it. "Go on."

Drew motioned that he was okay.

Molly shifted her weight and stared at the falls. "Mom and I were in this great spot. Like here, but everything was *more*." She waved her hands, sweeping out to encompass the sunlight and trees. "Like the light was super bright but didn't hurt your eyes. It was so amazing. So pretty. The colors around us were, well, way better than this, and this is a pretty nice spot. See how the water sparkles? Well . . . There the water was blue, green, white, shimmering, beautiful, pearly but somehow clear. Translucent. I can't get the right words to tell you."

Molly teared up, and Drew rushed to her side to comfort her.

She waved him away. "No, no. I'm fine. It just is so out of this world . . . I didn't want to leave. I wanted to stay there forever. Everything was love and color and light and happy. You could see the fish. They were so cool. The rainbow trout really had the colors of the rainbow. Every single blade of grass was separate but together, not like a lawn but in a living, giving way. It loved us, and the color was every shade of green imaginable and greener than that. I've never seen such jewel pure shades and tones. It . . . I don't have words for it . . . but it loved us, me, Mom. Everything was loving. I really would have stayed, you know."

Drew was silent for a long moment, then he gazed at her,

tears streaming down his cheeks. "I wouldn't have made it had you . . . I love you, and your mom entrusted you to my care . . ."

"Stop! It was up to *me*. The choice to stay or go was mine. There's a plan, and a hunk of a soulmate waiting for me, ya know. Mom told me. Well, she showed me. I can't tell you how. We could talk, but we didn't use our mouths, if that makes sense. Oh, none of this makes sense. But Mom said to tell you, *you* have a soulmate, too."

Drew laughed sheepishly. "Yeah, I know. I love her. Hear that, Dawn?"

Dawn froze at those words.

Molly giggled. "Silly me. Of course, you already know. You and Dawn saw the Ghost Stag. So did I, and so did my soulmate. For you, it's Dawn. Dawn and you. Yup. Mom said. So don't mess the plans up." She sighed. "Can we go now? I'm starving. Hospital food sucks."

Molly didn't want to discuss any more of her experience. It *was* heartbreaking, but not how or why the adults thought. *I can't put the whole thing into words. I know I died. I had to have. That must have been heaven, and the light was leading me forward. If I had gone any further, I would not have come back, and Marre — God, how I love her — wouldn't ever live. I know you get one soul. There's a plan. Marre has to be born, and I want to be with her and my soulmate, and this life here is the price. I know that. They think I'm grieving, but I can feel Mom. I know I'll see her again. But I can' tell anyone that ever. Well, maybe Jake when the time comes. I sure hope Uncle Drew and Dawn get it. They belong together.*

Chapter Fourteen: I Want to Know What Love Is

Dawn couldn't keep up with events. Time both compressed and expanded. COVID made it hard to even remember what day it was. But enough time had come and gone for Eve to have taken the drug cocktail and survive. She was even *discharged* from the field hospital.

Her worries eased now that Eve was doing so much better, but John's condition still weighed heavy on her mind. She had researched a procedure using convalescent plasma, where the antigens in a recovering patient could be given to another patient through transfusion. She discussed using the process with the doctors as an option to help John fight the coronavirus. They all agreed convalescent plasma had a possible chance of success.

Dawn approached Eve with the idea. "You know all that testing on you we've done?"

Eve nodded.

"You have enough antigens in your plasma that could help our father." She briefly explained the process, then added, "You share his blood type, so this may work."

"Go on," Eve prompted.

Dawn gave a half-smile and continued. "Our father doesn't look good. We're out of options, but if this it pans out, giving him your antigens, maybe . . ."

"Stop. No worries. I'll do it. But isn't it risky?"

Dawn shrugged. "Sometimes, the only option left is the scary one."

"Do it." Eve didn't even hesitate.

It took Dawn a couple of days of pulling a lot of strings, including at Veterans Administration, but she finally got the approval she needed to administer Eve's convalescent plasma to John.

She crossed her fingers and prayed. She noticed Marsha and Eve and everyone else around her doing the same thing.

By midafternoon, John woke, and Dawn could hardly believe the change in him. They took him off the ventilator, and his breathing kept improving throughout the day. She heaved a big sigh of relief and thanked God the procedure had worked.

Two days later, Dawn went with Eve to visit John. He was looking much better. She grabbed his chart to check his vitals. He wasn't completely out of the woods, but everything pointed to a full recovery.

"I'm doubly . . . blessed. You girls saved my llama," he said.

Eve grinned with tears in her eyes. "You gave us life, Dad."

Dawn squeezed his hand. "It was our turn to return the favor. Give you a second chance at life."

Dawn gave them a small salute and left the building.

Once outside, Dawn walked to the river behind the cabins for some much-needed alone time. *How do I reconcile what Molly told Drew and me? That's the question. Soulmates, seriously? The idea is ludicrous. Truly cray-cray, to borrow Molly's word for it. Even though Drew and I have managed to have some heart-stopping sex, I just don't know where to go from here. Is he the one meant for me? I know Drew loves me, and God help me, I love him right back. How could I not, after all we went through? Molly, Jake, John, Eve?*

Dawn couldn't afford to lose her career over a hot and heavy fling, if that was all it was. So, what if Molly had an NDE or near-death experience. It could have been a hallucination. However, what Molly reported was quite consistent with other stories they found in the NDE literature they buried themselves in every chance they got.

She took a deep breath and returned to the Lodge. She still had work to do.

The Great Smoky National Park was reopening. Dawn had discharged the last of her patients, who had some minor residual effects like fatigue and coughing but were otherwise doing well. They were ordered to return to their homes to isolate and recover. She smiled when John gave her a hug just before he walked out the door.

To date, she had not received any orders to pack up the field hospital, and she worried about that. It was likely to come down the pike if no dreaded second wave hit. However, COVID didn't care if the economy needed to recover. It struck wherever, whenever it could. She was already getting reports that the North and Midwest were reporting an increase of COVID cases. But the government had decided that tourism could resume, and judging by the traffic in town, tourists had shown up in droves. It was only a matter of time before she'd get her return orders.

What then? What about the new COVID cases here?

And what about Drew?

Drew wanted a future with her, but it was hard to find time to discuss anything. It even became impossible to find a place to be together and make love. She figured she'd have to take the bull by the horns and end this . . . this . . . what was it? An affair? No, it was way more than that.

Dawn used some of her new free time to get to know her new sisters and her father. Things looked to be working out good with her new family. John and Marsha were a hoot, and the Weathers' girls were just as bad as her and Eve.

She and Molly had created a fast, firm bond, and she knew she didn't want to lose that closeness. Still, she couldn't let her hormones lead her into troubled waters. She had to decide where her and Drew's relationship was going.

She texted Drew to meet her at the bonfire, hoping she'd have a solution by then. Drew's affirmative reply was immediate. He even included a heart emoji.

The day dragged. The more she wished time would fly by, the slower the clock seemed to move. Finally, night fell, and she walked to the firepit, her heart heavy.

When Drew spotted her, he rushed over, lifted her mask, and kissed her deeply. "We can't continue meeting like this."

Dawn wasn't really surprised by his words. They'd been stealing moments here and there to be together. "I know, right? Sneaking around like horny teenagers." She gazed up at him, choking back her tears. "I just can't do this anymore. It isn't ethical."

Drew ran a shaking hand down his bearded face and went down on one knee. "Then don't. Let's make it real and legal. Marry me, Dawn."

His reaction took her completely by surprise. The answer was right there in front of her, and she hadn't seen it coming. She could marry him! Fancy that. She'd have a family. Molly would be hers to guide and raise. She'd have her father and all her sisters. *A real family of my own at last!*

"I think I will," she teased with joy surging through her heart, almost overwhelming her.

"You will? I thought I'd have to force you to Jump the Broom, but . . . You will?"

"We can Jump the Broom and sweep the past away. Sweep my Daddy issue bye-bye." She laughed.

He had the good grace to cringe, but happiness won over. "It's hard to be romantic during a pandemic, but we can try." He pressed an app on his phone, and the song *I've Been*

Waiting for a Girl Like You played. He gathered her into his arms and danced her around in the firelight, dipped her, then gave her a long, deep, soul-searing kiss. "Marry me," he repeated.

From behind her, she suddenly heard clapping and hootin' and hollerin'. The others surrounded her. Her new family. Where had they all come from? Had Drew called in back up to convince her? She needed no convincing. Her heart wanted Drew.

Sunny pulled Eve and Beau forward. "I've got it. Get married here. Y'all can Jump the Broom, marry Southern Style like Skye did when she married Luke."

Sunny danced around with excitement, then squealed, "Let's do a double ceremony! Eve and Beau. You and Drew. Like Storme and I did. You can wear Gram's dress! Operation Double Ring!"

Storme jumped in. "Eve can wear my dress. We're practically quintuplets borne of different mothers."

Everyone looked at Storme, and she giggled. "You know what I'm sayin'."

Molly piped up. "Dibs on being Maid of Honor." She paused, looking back and forth, then smiled. "For both couples."

Eve looked at Beau.

He nodded.

Eve perked up. "I'll make sure your daisy wreath is perfect, Molly. To make up for Operation Panhandle, you know."

Dawn smiled at Drew, knowing that they would be jumping the broom in a very few days. Jumping into their new family. Then a thought struck, and she giggled.

Drew noticed and quickly asked, "What's wrong?"

She winked. "I'll be Dawn Sunrise."

Drew laughed. "I like the sound of that."

The End

KEEP AN EYE PEELED FOR MOUNTAIN DUE

Storme Knight longs for a baby of her own. She and Craig, feeling they lost so much time getting together after a tumultuous courtship, are finally ready for a child. But no matter what they do—standing on her head didn't work—no pregnancy results. They are willing to try just about anything. Are they desperate enough to take Sunny, her twin's, offer to become her surrogate seriously?

OTHER BOOKS BY KATHY

The Beach Series

Beyond the Beach 1
Beyond the Beach 2
Beyond the Beach 3
Beyond the Beach 4
Beyond the Beach 5

Back to the Beach 1
Back to the Beach 2

Promises on the Beach

The Mountain Series

Mountain Hot
Mountain Christmas
Mountain Skye Prequel, The Weather Girls
Mountain Joy
Mountain Kiss
Mountain Holly
Mountain Promises
Mountain Silver
Mountain Mistletoe
Mountain Bred
Mountain Led
Mountain Wed

Mountain Hookup
Mountain Fever
Mountain Due (Coming soon)

You may also enjoy the following from eXtasy Books Inc:

Promises on the Beach
Kathy Kalmar

Excerpt

Dean Chance Matthew's desk phone rang. He pressed talk.

"Zach is on line three," his secretary's voice announced.

He immediately picked up the receiver, and Zach started babbling before he even said hello.

"She's what?" Chance screeched. "Your mother isn't due yet."

"Sounds to me like she needs to go to the hospital," Zach, his thirteen-year-old stepson said.

Chance blew out a breath. In-out-in-out. Just like the birth classes taught us.

"It's three weeks too early!" He ran his hand through his slightly long hair. With the babies coming, he just hadn't had time to get a trim. If things had gone according to plan, he'd have kept his hair appointment. But the surprise baby shower had put the kibosh to that.

He was still dealing with the haul from the baby shower held the previous day. There was a ton of stuff to up pack, assemble, and put in place.

Caren can't be in labor now! His breathing was fast and shallow. He began to perspire. He wiped a hand across his sweaty forehead and noticed his hand was shaking. He inhaled, but letting the air out again was not as easy as actually doing it.

Calm down. Women have babies every day. But the woman having a baby this time wasn't just any woman. It was Caren, his love, his life, and she was having his baby—early! Snap out of it. Pay attention!

Zach was talking. "I know, but Mom said to call you, cuz it's happening now. Hurry up and get home."

"Okay. I'll be right there." He snatched his keys off the desk and barreled out the door, the receiver still in his grip. He pulled the phone off the desk in his hurry. It hit the floor with a bounce and disconnected. Shit! "My phone! Where the hell is my damn phone?"

His secretary, hearing the commotion, rushed into his office, grabbed his cell phone, handed it to him, and said in a dry tone, "In your hand now. Settle down. Babies are born every day. "

"My babies aren't!" Chance glanced at the cell phone and grinned. "Call my sister-in-law, Nikki Nolan. You have her number. Tell her to call Grandpa Gus, and Grandma Daisy, too."

"Done and done. They're all on their way over. Settle down. Drive safely."

Heart in his stomach, Chance Matthews sped home to his pregnant wife. Let them be okay. His first wife, Angie, and the baby she carried had died in a car accident. He could not lose Caren. Not after all we've been through. Hell, we've been through enough.

Chance had been ready to give up when Angie had died at the hands of a drunk driver. He had gone a little crazy then. It had been a daily struggle to keep going. For years afterward, he'd led a half-life. But he'd found a reason to live again after he met Caren on a Hawaiian vacation they had both won.

Caren had nearly drowned on that trip, getting caught by a rogue riptide. And if that wasn't enough, an erupting volcano had threatened Chance's life. They needed to catch a break. Chance only hoped God saw it his way. Please!

He pulled into their driveway as Nikki, Caren's sister, was getting out of her car.

Their adoptive grandparents, Gus and Daisy, were calming Emily, his stepdaughter, standing on the porch.

Caren stood next to them, gritting her teeth and holding her abdomen, obviously struggling to bite back screams as the pain doubled her over. Low groans escaped through her clenched lips.

"Take her and go," Gus said grimly. "Daisy and I have the kids, they'll be fine. Get out of here!"

Caren's pregnancy had been normal. Until this. She was approaching her mid-thirties, but she wasn't technically a high-risk pregnancy. If I lose her now . . . and the baby . . .

His wife struggled to give him a smile, but it came across more like a grimace.

Chance helped buckle her into the car while Nikki got into the back seat. Then he sped off, barely registering the stop sign as he barreled right through it. He took the next corner on two wheels and barely noticed the red light. Then, at last, he skidded to a stop in front of the emergency room entrance.

"I'm fine," Caren said. "Relax. Breathe. I gave birth early with both Zach and Emily."

"Are you trying to reassure me or you?"

"Both." She grinned.

The security attendant helped Caren into the nearby wheelchair while Chance dealt with the paperwork.

Mark Wheaton, his soon to be brother-in-law, met Chance on the maternity floor.

"Nikki joined Caren in the labor room," he told Mark, gesturing down the hallway. Chance again raked his hands through his hair as he paced the confines of the hall. A nurse finally showed up to take him to the labor room.

Someone was yelling at the top of her lungs. "Drugs! Give me drugs no matter what my birth plan says."

Chance winced and glanced at Mark. "Caren has a set of lungs on her." He would recognize her voice anywhere.

She had warned him she might cave in to the pain.

He wasn't allowed to let her give in. Those were his marching orders.

Nikki was not under those orders, so she dashed out of the room and went off to find someone who could help. She had been with Caren for the births of both Zach and Emily.

Caren had gone without drugs the first two times, but she was seven years older now.

Chance threw up his hands. Should I talk her off the ledge?

No one argued with her, but by the time Nikki found someone, the first baby had crowned. Drugs weren't an option any longer. They transferred Caren to the delivery room.

Chance accompanied her, stroking her arm, trying to support her.

Nikki followed shortly after she donned the hospital garb. She straightened her hair cover and appeared fully prepared to encourage and support both Chance and Caren.

"I have to push," Caren yelled.

Minutes later, at three-thirty-three in the afternoon, his newborn daughter quickly abandoned the birth canal and nearly flew into Chance's arms.

He sat there stunned. Don't fumble the ball, Matthews.

Calla Matthews had arrived in record time—less than four hours from first pain until the birth.

Two minutes later, Lily Matthews emerged crying lustily.

Caren, Chance, Calla, and Lily were all crying.

Oh my God, I'm a Dad!

Caren choked out, "Can you believe after all that angst about having a baby or not, we end up with twins?" She fell back on the delivery table looking wiped out, utterly spent. "Who'd believe it?"

"Hey, after all that's gone on, none of us has any business being surprised," Nikki answered.

The babies cried because it was what newborns did to use their new set of lungs and keep breathing, but the doctor pronounced them healthy and whole.

About the Author

Kathy Kalmar, born in Detroit, Michigan, lives with Larry, her husband of nearly four decades. Lately, she feels her life has recovered from the bad country song-like life because her Smoky Mountain Tops Round House is being rebuilt from the 2016 Chimney Tops II Wildfire. Her current residence is enlarged by four feet with the addition of their new puppy, Valentina. She loves to read and write contemporary romance novels. Meanwhile she remains fond of hot tubbing, chocolate, and sipping wine and mai tais and moonshine whether at home, Waikiki, Cape Cod or Tennessee. Y'all come back, hear? Currently, she is writing her next book. Aloha and Mahalo.

Contact Kathy at KathyKalmar.com

www.ingramcontent.com/pod-product-compliance
Lightning Source LLC
Chambersburg PA
CBHW070458130626
46555CB00003B/1065

* 9 781487 432171 *